Eros Unbound

ANAÏS NIN

Eros Unbound

GREAT LOVES

PENGUIN BOOKS

Published by the Penguin Group
Penguin Books Ltd, 80 Strand, London WC2R ORL, England
Penguin Group (USA) Inc., 375 Hudson Street, New York, New York 10014, USA
Penguin Group (Canada), 90 Eglinton Avenue East, Suite 700, Toronto, Ontario, Canada M4P 2Y3
(a division of Pearson Penguin Canada Inc.)
Penguin Ireland, 25 St Stephen's Green, Dublin 2, Ireland
(a division of Penguin Books Ltd)
Penguin Group (Australia), 250 Camberwell Road, Camberwell, Victoria 3124, Australia
(a division of Pearson Australia Group Pty Ltd)
Penguin Books India Pvt Ltd, 11 Community Centre, Panchsheel Park, New Delhi – 110 017, India
Penguin Group (NZ), 67 Apollo Drive, Rosedale, North Shore 0632, New Zealand
(a division of Pearson New Zealand Ltd)
Penguin Books (South Africa) (Pty) Ltd, 24 Sturdee Avenue,
Rosebank, Johannesburg 2196, South Africa

Penguin Books Ltd, Registered Offices: 80 Strand, London WC2R ORL, England

www.penguin.com

All stories apart from 'The Ring' and 'Linda' taken from *Little Birds* first published in
Great Britain by W. H. Allen & Co. 1979
Published in Penguin Books 1990
'The Ring' and 'Linda' taken from *Delta of Venus* first published in
Great Britain by W. H. Allen & Co. 1978
Published in Penguin Books 1990
This selection published in Penguin Books 2007

1

Typeset by Rowland Phototypesetting Ltd, Bury St Edmunds, Suffolk
Printed in England by Clays Ltd, St Ives plc

978-0-141-03292-4

Contents

1. The Maja — 1
2. The Woman on the Dunes — 7
3. Saffron — 17
4. A Model — 23
5. Hilda and Rango — 55
6. Two Sisters — 64
7. Linda — 79
8. The Ring — 102

Anaïs Nin (1903–1977) was a French-born author of Catalan, Cuban and Danish descent. She became famous for her erotica, as well as for her published diaries, which span more than sixty years, beginning when she was eleven years old and ending shortly before her death. She was born in Paris and spent her childhood in various parts of Europe. Her father left the family for another woman, which shocked Anaïs profoundly and was the reason for her mother to take her and her two brothers to live in the United States. Later Anaïs Nin moved to Paris with her husband, and they lived in France from 1924–1939, when Americans left on account of the war. She became acquainted with many well-known writers and artists, and wrote a series of novels and stories. In the 1940s she began to write erotica for an anonymous client, and these pieces are collected in *Delta of Venus* and *Little Birds* (both published posthumously), from which the stories in this collection are taken.

The Maja

The painter Novalis was newly married to María, a Spanish woman with whom he had fallen in love because she resembled the painting he most loved, the *Maja Desnuda*, by Goya.

They went to live in Rome. María clapped her hands in childish joy when she saw the bedroom, admiring the sumptuous Venetian furniture with its wonderful inlaid pearl and ebony.

That first night María, lying on a monumental bed made for the wife of a doge, trembled with delight, stretching her limbs before she hid them under the fine sheets. The pink toes of her plump feet moved as if they were calling Novalis.

But not once had she shown herself completely nude to her husband. First of all she was Spanish, then Catholic, then thoroughly bourgeois. Before lovemaking the light had to be put out.

Standing beside the bed, Novalis looked at her with his brows contracted, dominated by a desire that he hesitated to express; he wanted to see her, to admire her. He did not fully know her yet, despite those nights in the hotel when they could hear strange voices on the other side of the thin walls. What he asked was not the caprice of a lover, but the desire of a painter, of an artist. His eyes were hungry for her beauty.

María resisted, blushing, a trifle angry, her deepest prejudices offended.

'Don't be foolish, Novalis, dearest,' she said. 'Come to bed.'

But he persisted. She must overcome her bourgeois scruples, he said. Art scoffed at such modesty, human beauty was meant to be shown in all its majesty and not to be kept hidden, despised.

His hands, restrained by the fear of hurting her, gently pulled her weak arms, which were still crossed on her breast.

She laughed. 'You silly thing. You're tickling me. You're hurting me.'

But little by little, her feminine pride flattered by this worship of her body, she gave in to him, allowed herself to be treated like a child, with soft remonstrances, as if she were undergoing a pleasant torture.

Her body, freed from veils, shone with the whiteness of pearl. María closed her eyes as if she wanted to flee from the shame of her nakedness. On the smooth sheet, her graceful form intoxicated the eyes of the artist.

'You are Goya's fascinating little maja,' he said.

In the weeks that followed she would neither pose for him nor allow him to use models. She would appear unexpectedly in his studio and chat with him while he painted. One afternoon when she came suddenly into the studio she saw on the model's platform a naked woman lying in some furs, showing the curves of her ivory back.

Later María made a scene. Novalis begged her to

pose for him; she capitulated. Tired out by the heat, she fell asleep. He worked for three hours without a pause.

With frank immodesty, she admired herself in the canvas just as she did in the great mirror in the bedroom. Dazzled by the beauty of her own body, she momentarily lost her self-consciousness. Also, Novalis had painted a different face on her body so that no one would recognize her.

But afterwards, María fell again into her old habits of thinking, refused to pose. She made a scene each time Novalis engaged a model, watching and listening behind doors and quarreling constantly.

She became quite ill with anxiety and morbid fears and developed insomnia. The doctor gave her pills which sent her off into a deep sleep.

Novalis noticed that when she took these pills she did not hear him get up, move about, or even spill objects in the room. One morning he awakened early, with the intention of working, and watched her sleep, so deeply that she rarely stirred at all. A strange idea occurred to him.

He drew back the sheets that covered her, and slowly began to lift up her silk nightgown. He was able to raise it above her breasts without her giving any sign of awakening. Now her whole body lay exposed and he could contemplate it as long as he wanted. Her arms were flung outwards; her breasts lay under his eyes like an offering. He was roused with desire for her but still did not dare touch her. Instead he brought his drawing paper and pencils, sat at her side and sketched her. As he worked, he had the feeling he was caressing each perfect line in her body.

He was able to continue for two hours. When he observed the effect of the sleeping pills beginning to wear off, he pulled down her nightgown, covered her with the sheet and left the room.

Later, María was surprised to notice a new enthusiasm for work in her husband. He locked himself in his studio for whole days, painting from the pencil sketches he made in the mornings.

In this way he completed several paintings of her, always reclining, always asleep, as she had been on the first day she posed. María was amazed by his obsession. She thought it was merely a repetition of the first pose. He always altered her face. Since her actual expression was forbidding and severe, no one who saw these paintings ever imagined that the voluptuous body was that of María.

Novalis no longer desired his wife when she was awake, with her puritanical expression and stern eyes. He desired her when she was asleep, abandoned, rich and soft.

He painted her without respite. When he was alone with a new painting in his studio, he lay on the couch in front of it, and then a warmth ran through his whole body, as his eyes rested on the maja's breasts, on the valley of her belly, on the hair between her legs. He began to feel an erection stirring. He was surprised at the violent effect of the painting.

One morning he stood in front of María as she lay sleeping. He had succeeded in parting her legs slightly, so as to see the line between them. Watching her unconstrained pose, her opened legs, he fingered his sex with the illusion that she was doing it. How often he had led her hand to his penis, trying to obtain this caress from her, but she was always repulsed and moved her hand away. Now he enclosed his penis fully in his own strong hand.

María soon realized she had lost his love. She did not know how to win it back. She became aware that he was in love with her body only as he painted it.

She went to the country to stay with friends for a week. But after a few days she fell ill and returned home to see her doctor. When she arrived at the house it looked uninhabited. She tiptoed to Novalis's studio. There was no sound. Then she began to imagine that he was making love to a woman. She approached the door. Slowly and noiselessly, like a thief, she opened it. And this is what she saw: on the floor of the studio, a painting of herself; and lying over it, rubbing himself against it, her husband, naked, with his hair wild, as she had never seen him, his penis erect.

He moved against the painting lasciviously, kissing it, fondling it between the legs. He lay against it as he never had against her. He seemed driven into a frenzy, and all around him were the other paintings of her, nude, voluptuous, beautiful. He threw a passionate glance at them and continued his imaginary embrace. It was an orgy with her he was having, with a wife he had not known in reality. At the sight of this, María's own controlled sensuality flared up, free for the first time. When she took off her clothes, she revealed a

María new to him, a María illumined with passion, abandoned as in the paintings, offering her body shamelessly, without hesitation to all his embraces, striving to efface the paintings from his emotions, to surpass them.

The Woman on the Dunes

Louis could not sleep. He turned over in his bed to lie on his stomach and, burying his face in the pillow, moved against the hot sheets as if he were lying over the woman. But when the friction increased the fever in his body, he stopped himself.

He got out of his bed and looked at his watch. It was two o'clock. What could he do to appease his fever? He left his studio. The moon was shining and he could see the roads clearly. The place, a beach town in Normandy, was full of little cottages, which people could rent for the night or a week. Louis wandered aimlessly.

Then he saw that one of the cottages was lighted. It was set into the woods, isolated. It intrigued him that anyone should be up so late. He approached it soundlessly, his footsteps lost in the sand. The Venetian blinds were down but not tightly closed, so he could see right into the room. And his eyes met the most amazing sight: a very wide bed, profusely covered with pillows and rumpled blankets, as if it had already been the scene of a great battle; a man, seemingly cornered in a pile of pillows, as if pushed there after a series of attacks, reclining like a pasha in a harem, very calm and contented, naked, his legs folded out; and a woman, also naked, whom Louis could see only from the back, contorting herself before this pasha, undulating and deriving such pleasure from whatever she was doing with her head between his legs that her ass would shake tremulously, her legs tighten as if she were about to leap.

Now and then the man placed his hand over her head as if to restrain her frenzy. He tried to move away. Then she leaped with great agility and placed herself over him, kneeling over his face. He no longer moved. His face was directly under her sex, which, her stomach curved outwards, she held before him.

As he was pinned under her, she was the one to move within reach of his mouth, which had not touched her yet. Louis saw the man's sex rise and lengthen, and he tried with an embrace to bring her down upon him. But she remained at a short distance, looking, enjoying the spectacle of her own beautiful stomach and hair and sex so near to his mouth.

Then slowly, slowly she moved towards him and, with her head bowed, watched the melting of his mouth between her legs.

For a long while they maintained this position. Louis was in such a turmoil that he left the window. Had he remained longer he would have had to throw himself on the ground and somehow satisfy his burning desire, and this he did not want to do.

He began to feel that in every cottage something was taking place that he would like to be sharing. He walked faster, haunted by the image of the man and woman, the round firm belly of the woman as she arched herself over the man . . .

Then he reached the sand dunes and complete solitude. The dunes shone like snowy hills in the clear night. Behind them lay the ocean, whose rhythmic movements he could hear. He walked in the white moonlight. And then he caught sight of a figure walking before him, walking fast and lightly. It was a woman. She wore some kind of cape, which the wind billowed like a sail, and seemed propelled by it. He would never catch up with her.

She was walking towards the ocean. He followed her. They walked in the snowlike dunes for a long while. At the ocean's edge, she flung off her clothes and stood naked in the summer night. She ran into the surf. And Louis, in imitation, discarded his clothes and ran into the water also. Only then did she see him. At first she was still. But when she saw his young body clearly in the moonlight, his fine head, his smile, she was not frightened. He swam towards her. They smiled at each other. His smile, even at night, was dazzling; hers, too. They could scarcely distinguish anything but the brilliant smiles and the outlines of their perfect bodies.

He came closer to her. She let him. Suddenly he swam deftly and gracefully over her body, touching it, and passing on.

She continued to swim, and he repeated his passage over her. Then she stood up, and he dove down and passed between her legs. They laughed. They both moved with ease in the water.

He was deeply excited. He swam with his sex hard. Then they approached each other with a crouching motion, as if for a battle. He brought her body against his, and she felt the tautness of his penis.

He placed it between her legs. She touched it. His hands searched her, caressed her everywhere. Then again she moved away, and he had to swim to catch her. Again his penis lay lightly between her legs, then he pressed her more firmly against him and sought to penetrate her. She broke loose and ran out of the water, into the sand dunes. Dripping, shining, laughing, he ran after her. The warmth of the running set him on fire again. She fell on the sand, and he over her.

Then at the moment when he most desired her, his power suddenly failed him. She lay waiting for him, smiling and moist, and his desire wilted. Louis was baffled. He had been in a state of desire for days. He wanted to take this woman and he couldn't. He was deeply humiliated.

Strangely enough, her voice grew tender. 'There is plenty of time,' she said. 'Don't move away. It's lovely.'

Her warmth passed into him. His desire did not return, but it was sweet to feel her. Their bodies lay together, his belly against hers, his sexual hair brushing against hers, her breasts pointed at his chest, her mouth glued to his.

Then slowly he slipped off to look at her – her long, slender, polished legs, her rich pubic hair, her lovely pale glowing skin, her full breasts very high, her long hair, her wide smiling mouth.

He was sitting like a Buddha. She leaned over and took his small wilted penis in her mouth. She licked it softly, tenderly, lingering over the tip of it. It stirred.

He looked down at the sight of her wide red mouth so beautifully curved around his penis. With one hand she touched his balls, with the other she moved the head of the penis, enclosing it and pulling it gently.

Then, sitting against him, she took it and directed it between her legs. She rubbed the penis gently against her clitoris, over and over again. Louis watched the hand, thinking how beautiful it looked, holding the penis as if it were a flower. It stirred but did not harden sufficiently to enter her.

He could see at the opening of her sex the moisture of her desire appearing, glistening in the moonlight. She continued to rub. The two bodies, equally beautiful, were bent over this rubbing motion, the small penis feeling the touch of her skin, her warm flesh, enjoying the friction.

She said, 'Give me your tongue,' and leaned over. Without interrupting the rubbing of his penis, she took his tongue in her mouth and touched the tip of it with her own tongue. Each time the penis touched her clitoris, her tongue touched the tip of his tongue. And Louis felt the warmth running between his tongue and his penis, running back and forth.

In a husky voice she said, 'Stick your tongue out, out.'

He obeyed her. She again cried, 'Out, out, out, out . . .' obsessively, and when he did so he felt such a stirring through his body, as if it were his penis extending towards her, to reach into her.

She kept her mouth open, two slender fingers around his penis, her legs parted, expectantly.

Louis felt a turmoil, the blood running through his body and down to his penis. It hardened.

The woman waited. She did not take in his penis at once. She let him, now and then, touch his tongue against hers. She let him pant like a dog in heat, open his being, stretch towards her. He looked at the red mouth of her sex, open and waiting, and suddenly the violence of his desire shook him, completed the hardening of the penis. He threw himself over her, his tongue inside of her mouth, and his penis pressing inside of her.

But again he could not come. They rolled together for a long while. Finally they got up and walked, carrying their clothes. Louis's sex was stretched and taut, and she delighted in the sight. Now and then they fell on the sand, and he took her, and churned her, and left her, moist and hot. And as they again walked, she in front of him, he encircled her in his arms, and threw her on the ground so that they were like dogs coupling, on their hands and knees. He shook inside of her, pushed and vibrated, and kissed her, and held her breasts in his hands.

'Do you want it? Do you want it?' he asked.

'Yes, give it to me, but make it last, do not come; I like it like this, over and over and over again.'

She was so moist and feverish. She would walk, waiting for the moment he would thrust her into the sand and take her again, stirring her and then leaving her before she had come. Each time, she felt anew his hands over her body, the warm sand against her skin, his caressing mouth, the caressing wind.

As they walked, she took his erect penis into her hand. Once she stopped him, knelt before him and held it in her mouth. He stood towering over her, with his belly moving slightly forwards. Another time she pressed his penis between her breasts, making a cushion for it, holding it and letting it glide between this soft embrace. Dizzy, palpitating, vibrating from these caresses, they walked drunkenly.

Then they saw a house and stopped. He begged her to conceal herself among the bushes. He wanted to come; he would not leave her until then. She was so aroused and yet she wanted to hold back and wait for him.

This time when he was inside of her he began shaking, and finally he came, with a violence. She half climbed over his body to reach her own fulfillment. They cried together.

Lying back, resting, smoking, with the dawn coming upon them, lighting their faces, they now felt too cool and covered their bodies with their clothes. The woman, looking away from Louis, told him a story.

She had been in Paris when they had hanged a Russian radical who had killed a diplomat. She was then living in Montparnasse, frequenting the cafés, and she had followed the trial with a passion, as all her friends had done, because the man was a fanatic, had given Dostoevskian answers to the questions put to him, faced the trial with great religious courage.

At that time they still executed people for grave offenses. It usually took place at dawn, when no one was about, in a little square near the prison of the

Santé, where the guillotine had stood at the time of the Revolution. And one could not get very near, because of the police guard. Few people attended these hangings. But in the case of the Russian, because emotions had been so much aroused, all the students and artists of Montparnasse, the young agitators and revolutionaries, had decided to attend. They waited up all night, getting drunk.

She had waited with them, had drunk with them, and was in a great state of excitement with fear. It was the first time she was to see someone die. It was the first time she was to see someone hanged. It was the first time she was to witness a scene that had been repeated many, many times during the Revolution.

Towards dawn, the crowd moved to the square, as near as the rope, stretched by the policemen, would allow and gathered in a circle. She was carried by the waves of crowding and pushing people to a spot about ten meters away from the scaffold.

There she stood, pressed against the rope, watching with fascination and terror. Then a stirring in the crowd pushed her away from her position. Still, she could see by standing on her toes. People were crushing her from all sides. The prisoner was brought in with his eyes blindfolded. The hangman stood by, waiting. Two policemen held the man and slowly led him up the stairs to the scaffold.

At this moment she became aware of someone pressing against her far more eagerly than necessary. In the trembling, excited condition she was in, the pressure was not disagreeable. Her body was in a fever.

Anyway, she could scarcely move, so pinned was she to the spot by the curious crowd.

She wore a white blouse and a skirt that buttoned all the way down the side as was the fashion then – a short skirt and a blouse through which one could see her rosy underwear and guess at the shape of her breasts.

Two hands encircled her waist, and she distinctly felt a man's body, his desire hard against her ass. She held her breath. Her eyes were fixed on the man who was about to be hanged, which made her body painfully nervous, and at the same time the hands reached for her breasts and pressed upon them.

She felt dizzy with conflicting sensations. She did not move or turn her head. A hand now sought an opening in the skirt and discovered the buttons. Each button undone by the hand made her gasp with both fear and relief. The hand waited to see if she protested before proceeding to another button. She did not move.

Then, with a dexterity and swiftness she had not expected, the two hands twisted her skirt round so that the opening was at the back. In the heaving crowd, now all she could feel was a penis slowly being slipped into the opening of her skirt.

Her eyes remained fixed on the man who was mounting the scaffold, and with each beat of her heart the penis gained headway. It had traversed the skirt and parted the slit in her panties. How warm and firm and hard it was against her flesh. The condemned man stood on the scaffold now and the noose was put around his neck. The pain of watching him was so great that it made this touch of flesh a relief, a human, warm, consoling thing. It seemed to her then that his penis quivering between her buttocks was something wonderful to hold on to, life, life to hold while death was passing . . .

Without saying a word, the Russian bowed his head in the noose. Her body trembled. The penis advanced between the soft folds of her buttocks, pushed its way inexorably into her flesh.

She was palpitating with fear, and it was like the palpitation of desire. As the condemned man was flung into space and death, the penis gave a great leap inside of her, gushing out its warm life.

The crowd crushed the man against her. She almost ceased breathing, and, as her fear became pleasure, wild pleasure at feeling life while a man was dying, she fainted.

After this story Louis dozed off to sleep. When he awakened, saturated with sensual dreams, vibrating from some imaginary embrace, he saw that the woman had gone. He could follow her footprints along the sand for quite a distance, but they disappeared in the wooded section that led to the cottages, and so he lost her.

Saffron

Fay had been born in New Orleans. When she was sixteen she was courted by a man of forty whom she had always liked for his aristocracy and distinction. Fay was poor. Albert's visits were events to her family. For him their poverty was hastily disguised. He came very much like the liberator, talking about a life Fay had never known, at the other end of the city.

When they were married, Fay was installed like a princess in his house, which was hidden in an immense park. Handsome colored women waited on her. Albert treated her with extreme delicacy.

The first night he did not take her. He maintained that this was proof of love, not to force oneself upon one's wife, but to woo her slowly and lingeringly, until she was prepared and in the mood to be possessed.

He came to her room and merely caressed her. They lay enveloped in the white mosquito netting as within a bridal veil, lay back in the hot night fondling and kissing. Fay felt languid and drugged. He was giving birth to a new woman with every kiss, exposing a new sensibility. Afterwards, when he left her, she lay tossing and unable to sleep. It was as if he had started tiny fires under her skin, tiny currents which kept her awake.

She was exquisitely tormented in this manner for

several nights. Being inexperienced, she did not try to bring about a complete embrace. She yielded to this profusion of kisses in her hair, on her neck, shoulders, arms, back, legs . . . Albert took delight in kissing her until she moaned, as if he were now sure of having awakened a particular part of her flesh, and then his mouth moved on.

He discovered the trembling sensibility under the arm, at the nascence of the breasts, the vibrations that ran between the nipples and the sex, and between the sex mouth and the lips, all the mysterious links that roused and stirred places other than the one being kissed, currents running from the roots of the hair to the roots of the spine. Each place he kissed he worshiped with adoring words, observing the dimples at the end of her back, the firmness of her buttocks, the extreme arch of her back, which threw her buttocks outwards – 'like a colored woman's', he said.

He encircled her ankles with his fingers, lingered over her feet, which were perfect like her hands, stroked over and over again the smooth statuesque lines of her neck, lost himself in her long heavy hair.

Her eyes were long and narrow like those of a Japanese woman, her mouth full, always half-open. Her breasts heaved as he kissed her and marked her shoulder's sloping line with his teeth. And then as she moaned, he left her, closing the white netting around her carefully, encasing her like a treasure, leaving her with the moisture welling up between her legs.

One night, as usual, she could not sleep. She sat up in her clouded bed, naked. As she rose to look for her

kimono and slippers a tiny drop of honey fell from her
sex, rolled down her leg, stained the white rug. Fay
was baffled at Albert's control, his reserve. How could
he subdue his desire and sleep after these kisses and
caresses? He had not even completely undressed. She
had not seen his body.

She decided to leave her room and walk until she
could become calm again. Her entire body was throb-
bing. She walked slowly down the wide staircase and
out into the garden. The perfume of the flowers almost
stunned her. The branches fell languidly over her and
the mossy paths made her footsteps absolutely silent.
She had the feeling that she was dreaming. She walked
aimlessly for a long while. And then a sound startled
her. It was a moan, a rhythmic moan like a woman's
complaining. The light from the moon fell there
between the branches and exposed a colored woman
lying naked on the moss and Albert over her. Her
moans were moans of pleasure. Albert was crouching
like a wild animal and pounding against her. He, too,
was uttering confused cries; and Fay saw them convulsed under her very eyes by the violent joys.

Neither one saw Fay. She did not cry out. The pain
at first paralyzed her. Then she ran back to the house,
filled with all the humility of her youth, of her inexperi-
ence; she was tortured with doubts of herself. Was it
her fault? What had she lacked, what had she failed to
do to please Albert? Why had he had to leave her and
go to the colored woman? The savage scene haunted
her. She blamed herself for falling under the enchantment of his caresses and perhaps not acting as

he wanted her to. She felt condemned by her own femininity.

Albert could have taught her. He had said he was wooing her . . . waiting. He had only to whisper a few words. She was ready to obey. She knew he was older and she innocent. She had expected to be taught.

That night Fay became a woman, making a secret of her pain, intent on saving her happiness with Albert, on showing wisdom and subtlety. When he lay at her side she whispered to him, 'I wish you would take your clothes off.'

He seemed startled, but he consented. Then she saw his youthful, slim body at her side, with his very white hair gleaming, a curious mingling of youth and age. He began to kiss her. As he did so, her hand timidly moved towards his body. At first she was frightened. She touched his chest. Then his hips. He continued to kiss her. Her hand reached for his penis, slowly. He made a movement away from it. It was soft. He moved away and began to kiss her between the legs. He was whispering over and over again the same phrase, 'You have the body of an angel. It is impossible that such a body should have a sex. You have the body of an angel.'

Then anger swept over Fay like a fever, an anger at his moving his penis away from her hand. She sat up, her hair wild about her shoulders, and said, 'I am not an angel, Albert. I am a woman. I want you to love me as a woman.'

Then came the saddest night Fay had ever known, because Albert tried to possess her and he couldn't. He led her hands to caress. His penis would harden, he would begin to place it between her legs, and then it would wilt in her hands.

He was tense, silent. She could see the torment on his face. He tried many times. He would say, 'Just wait a little while, just wait.' He said this so humbly, so gently. Fay lay there, it seemed to her, for the whole of the night, wet, desirous, expectant, and all night he made half-finished assaults on her, failing, retreating, kissing her as if in atonement. Then Fay sobbed.

This scene was repeated for two or three nights, and then Albert no longer came to her room.

And almost every day Fay saw shadows in the garden, shadows embracing. She was afraid to move from her room. The house was completely carpeted and noiseless, and, as she walked up the stairs once, she caught sight of Albert climbing behind one of the colored girls and running his hand under her voluminous skirt.

Fay became obsessed with the sounds of the moaning. It seemed to her that she heard it continuously. Once she went to the colored girls' rooms, which were in a separate little house, and listened. She could hear the moans she had heard in the park. She broke into tears. A door opened. It was not Albert who came out but one of the colored gardeners. He found Fay sobbing there.

Eventually Albert took her, under the most unusual circumstances. They were going to give a party for Spanish friends. Although she seldom shopped, Fay went to the city to get a particular saffron for the rice, a very extraordinary brand that had just arrived on a ship from Spain. She enjoyed buying the saffron, freshly unloaded. She had always liked smells, the smells of the wharves, and warehouses. When the little packages of saffron were handed to her, she tucked them in her bag, which she carried against her breast, under her arm. The smell was powerful, it seeped into her clothes, her hands, her very body.

When she arrived home Albert was waiting for her. He came towards the car and lifted her out of it, playfully, laughing. As he did so, she brushed with her full weight against him and he exclaimed, 'You smell of saffron!'

She saw a curious brilliance in his eyes, as he pressed his face against her breasts, smelling her. Then he kissed her. He followed her into her bedroom, where she threw her bag on the bed. The bag opened. The smell of saffron filled the room. Albert made her lie on the bed, fully dressed, and without kisses or caresses, took her.

Afterwards he said happily, 'You smell like a colored woman.' And the spell was broken.

A Model

My mother had European ideas about young girls. I was sixteen. I had never gone out alone with young men, I had never read anything but literary novels, and by choice I never was like girls my own age. I was what you would call a sheltered person, very much like some Chinese woman, instructed in the art of making the most of the discarded dresses sent to me by a rich cousin, singing and dancing, writing elegantly, reading the finest books, conversing intelligently, arranging my hair beautifully, keeping my hands white and delicate, using only the refined English I had learned since my arrival from France, dealing with everybody in terms of great politeness.

This was what was left of my European education. But I was very much like the Orientals in one other way: long periods of gentleness were followed by bursts of violence, taking the form of temper and rebellion or of quick decision and positive action.

I suddenly decided to go to work, without consulting anybody or asking anybody's approval. I knew my mother would be against my plan.

I had rarely gone to New York alone. Now I walked the streets, answering all kinds of advertisements. My accomplishments were not very practical. I knew languages but not typewriting. I knew Spanish dancing but not the new ballroom dances. Everywhere I went I did not inspire confidence. I looked even younger than my age and over-delicate, over-sensitive. I looked as if I could not bear any burdens put on me, yet this was only an appearance.

After a week I had obtained nothing but a sense of not being useful to anyone. It was then I went to see a family friend who was very fond of me. She had disapproved of my mother's way of protecting me. She was happy to see me, amazed at my decision and willing to help me. It was while talking to her humorously about myself, enumerating my assets, that I happened to say that a painter had come to see us the week before and had said that I had an exotic face. My friend jumped up.

'I have it,' she said. 'I know what you can do. It is true that you have an unusual face. Now I know an art club where artists go for their models. I will introduce you there. It is a sort of protection for the girls, instead of having them walk about from studio to studio. The artists are registered at the club, where they are known, and they telephone when they need a model.'

When we arrived at the club on Fifty-seventh Street, there was great animation and many people. It turned out that they were preparing for the annual show. Every year all the models were dressed in costumes that best suited them and exhibited to the painters. I was quickly registered for a small fee and was sent upstairs to two elderly ladies who took me into the costume room. One of them chose an eighteenth-century costume. The other fixed my hair above my ears. They taught me how to wax my eyelashes. I saw a new self in the mirrors. The rehearsal was going on. I had to walk downstairs and stroll around the room. It was not difficult. It was like a masquerade ball.

The day of the show everyone was rather nervous. Much of a model's success depended on this event. My hand trembled as I made up my eyelashes. I was given a rose to carry, which made me feel a little ridiculous. I was received with applause. After all the girls had walked slowly around the room, the painters talked with us, took down our names, made engagements. My engagement book was filled like a dance card.

Monday at nine o'clock I was to be at the studio of a well-known painter; at one, at the studio of an illustrator; at four, at the studio of a miniaturist, and so on. There were women painters too. They objected to our using make-up. They said that when they engaged a made-up model and then got her to wash her face before posing, she did not look the same. For that reason posing for women did not attract us very much.

My announcement at home that I was a model came like a thunderbolt. But it was done. I could make twenty-five dollars a week. My mother wept a little, but was pleased deep down.

That night we talked in the dark. Her room connected with mine and the door was open. My mother was worrying about what I knew (or did not know) about sex.

The sum of my knowledge was this: that I had been kissed many times by Stephen, lying on the sand at the beach. He had been lying over me, and I had felt something bulky and hard pressing against me, but that was all, and to my great amazement when I came home I had discovered that I was all wet between the legs. I had not mentioned this to my mother. My private impression was that I was a great sensualist, that this getting wet between the legs at being kissed showed dangerous tendencies for the future. In fact, I felt quite like a whore.

My mother asked me, 'Do you know what happens when a man takes a woman?'

'No,' I said, 'but I would like to know *how* a man takes a woman in the first place.'

'Well, you know the small penis you saw when you bathed your brother – that gets big and hard and the man pushes it inside of the woman.'

That seemed ugly to me. 'It must be difficult to get it in,' I said.

'No, because the woman gets wet before that, so it slides in easily.'

Now I understood the mystery of wetness.

In that case, I thought to myself, I will never get raped, because to get wet you have to like the man.

A few months before, having been violently kissed in the woods by a big Russian who was bringing me home from a dance, I had come home and announced that I was pregnant.

Now I remembered how one night when several of us were returning from another dance, driving along the speedway, we had heard girls screaming. My escort, John, stopped the car. Two girls ran to us from the bushes, disheveled, dresses torn and eyes haggard. We let them into the car. They were mumbling chaotically about having been taken for a ride on a motorcycle and then attacked. One of them kept saying: 'If he broke through, I'll kill myself.'

John stopped at an inn and I took the girls to the ladies' room. They immediately went into the toilet together. One was saying: 'There is no blood. I guess he didn't break through.' The other one was crying.

We took them home. One of the girls thanked me and said, 'I hope that never happens to you.'

While my mother was talking, I was wondering if she feared this and was preparing me.

I cannot say that when Monday came I was not uneasy. I felt that if the painter was attractive I would be in greater danger than if he was not, for if I liked him I might get wet between the legs.

The first one was about fifty, bald, with a rather European face and a little mustache. He had a beautiful studio.

He placed the screen in front of me so that I could change my dress. I threw my clothes over the screen. As I threw my last piece of underwear over the top of the screen, I saw the painter's face appear at the top, smiling. But it was done so comically and ridiculously, like a scene in a play, that I said nothing, got dressed and took the pose.

Every half-hour I would get a rest. I could smoke a cigarette. The painter put on a record and said: 'Will you dance?'

We danced on the highly polished floor, turning among the paintings of beautiful women. At the end

of the dance, he kissed my neck. 'So dainty,' he said.
'Do you pose in the nude?'

'No.'

'Too bad.'

I thought this was not so difficult to manage. It was
time to pose again. The three hours passed quickly. He
talked while he worked. He said he had married his
first model; that she was unbearably jealous; that every
now and then she broke into the studio and made
scenes; that she would not let him paint from the nude.
He had rented another studio she did not know about.
Often he worked there. He gave parties there too.
Would I like to come to one on Saturday night?

He gave me another little kiss on the neck as I left.
He winked and said: 'You won't tell the club on me?'

I returned to the club for luncheon because I could
make up my face and freshen myself, and they gave
us a cheap lunch. The other girls were there. We fell
into conversation. When I mentioned the invitation for
Saturday night, they laughed, nodding at one another. I
could not get them to talk. One girl had lifted up her
skirt and was examining a mole way up her thighs.
With a little caustic pencil she was trying to burn it
away. I saw that she was not wearing panties, just a
black satin dress which clung to her. The telephone
would ring and then one of the girls would be called
and go off to work.

The next was a young illustrator. He was wearing
his shirt open at the neck. He did not move when I
came in. He shouted at me, 'I want to see a lot of
back and shoulders. Put a shawl around yourself or

something.' Then he gave me a small old-fashioned umbrella and white gloves. The shawl he pinned down almost to my waist. This was for a magazine cover.

The arrangement of the shawl over my breasts was precarious. As I tilted my head at the angle he wanted, in a sort of inviting gesture, the shawl slipped and my breasts showed. He would not let me move. 'Wish I could paint them in,' he said.

He was smiling as he worked with his charcoal pencil. Leaning over to measure me, he touched the tips of my breasts with his pencil and made a little black mark. 'Keep that pose,' he said as he saw me ready to move. I kept it.

Then he said: 'You girls sometimes act as if you thought you were the only ones with breasts or asses. I see so many of them they don't interest me, I assure you. I take my wife all dressed always. The more clothes she has on the better. I turn off the light. I know too much how women are made. I've drawn millions of them.'

The little touch of the pencil on my breasts had hardened the tips. This angered me, because I had not felt it a pleasure at all. Why were my breasts so sensitive, and did he notice it?

He went on drawing and coloring his picture. He stopped to drink whiskey and offered me some. He dipped his finger in the whiskey and touched one of my nipples. I was not posing so I moved away angrily. He kept smiling at me. 'Doesn't it feel nice?' he said. 'It warms them.'

It was true that the tips were hard and red.

'Very nice nipples you have. You don't need to use lipstick on them, do you? They are naturally rosy. Most of them have a leather color.'

I covered myself.

That was all for that day. He asked me to come the next day at the same time.

He was slower in getting to his work on Tuesday. He talked. He had his feet up on his drawing table. He offered me a cigarette. I was pinning up my shawl. He was watching me. He said: 'Show me your legs. I may do a drawing of legs next time.'

I lifted up my skirt above the knee.

'Sit down with your skirt up high,' he said.

He sketched in the legs. There was a silence.

Then he got up, flung his pencil on the table, leaned over me and kissed me fully on the mouth, forcing my head backwards. I pushed him off violently. This made him smile. He slipped his hand swiftly up under my skirt, felt my thighs where the stockings stopped and before I could move was back in his seat.

I took the pose and said nothing, because I had just made a discovery – that in spite of my anger, in spite of the fact that I was not in love, the kiss and the caress on the naked thighs had given me pleasure. While I fought him off, it was only out of habit, but actually it had given me pleasure.

The pose gave me time to awaken from the pleasure and remember my defenses. But my defenses had been convincing and he was quiet for the rest of the morning.

From the very first I had divined that what I really had to defend myself against was my own susceptibility to caresses. I was also filled with great curiosities about so many things. At the same time I was utterly convinced that I would not give myself to anyone but the man I fell in love with.

I was in love with Stephen. I wanted to go to him and say: 'Take me, take me!' I suddenly remembered another incident, and that was a year before this when one of my aunts had taken me to New Orleans to the Mardi Gras. Friends of hers had driven us in their automobile. There were two other young girls with us. A band of young men took advantage of the confusion, the noise, the excitement and gaiety to jump into our automobile, remove our masks and begin kissing us while my aunt raised an outcry. Then they disappeared into the crowd. I was left dazed and wishing that the young man who had taken hold of me and had kissed me on the mouth were still there. I was languid from the kiss, languid and stirred.

Back at the club I wondered what all the rest of the models felt. There was a great deal of talk about defending oneself, and I wondered whether it was all sincere. One of the loveliest models, whose face was not particularly beautiful but who had a magnificent body, was talking:

'I don't know what other girls feel about posing in the nude,' she said, 'I love it. Ever since I was a little girl I liked taking off my clothes. I liked to see how people looked at me. I used to take my clothes off at parties, as soon as people were a little drunk. I liked showing my body. Now I can't wait to take them off. I enjoy being looked at. It gives me pleasure. I get shivers of pleasure right down my back when men look at me. And when I pose for a whole class of artists at the school, when I see all those eyes on my body, I get so much pleasure, it is – well, it is like being made love to. I feel beautiful, I feel as women must feel sometimes when undressed for a lover. I enjoy my own body. I like to pose holding my breasts in my hand. Sometimes I caress them. I was once in burlesque. I loved it. I enjoyed doing that as much as the men enjoyed seeing it. The satin of the dress used to give me shivers – taking my breasts out, exposing myself. That excited me. When men touched me I did not get as much excitement . . . it was always a disappointment. But I know other girls who don't feel that way.'

'I feel humiliated,' said a red-haired model. 'I feel my body is not my own, and that it no longer has any value . . . being seen by everybody.'

'I don't feel anything at all,' said another. 'I feel it's all impersonal. When men are painting or drawing, they no longer think of us as human beings. One painter told me that the body of a model on the stand is an objective thing, that the only moment he felt disturbed erotically was when the model took off her kimono. In Paris, they tell me, the model undresses right in front of the class, and that's exciting.'

'If it were all so objective,' said another girl, 'they wouldn't invite us to parties afterwards.'

'Or marry their models,' I added, remembering two painters I had already met who had married their favorite models.

*

One day I had to pose for an illustrator of stories. When I arrived, I found two other people already there, a girl and a man. We were to compose scenes together, love scenes for a romance. The man was about forty, with a very mature, very decadent face. It was he who knew how to arrange us. He placed me in a position for a kiss. We had to hold the pose while the illustrator photographed us. I was uneasy. I did not like the man at all. The other girl played the jealous wife who burst in on the scene. We had to do it many times. Each time the man acted the kiss I shrank inside myself, and he felt it. He was offended. His eyes were mocking. I acted badly. The illustrator was shouting at me as if we were in a moving picture, 'More passion, put more passion into it!'

I tried to remember how the Russian had kissed me on returning from the dance, and that relaxed me. The man repeated the kiss. And now I felt he was holding me closer than he needed to, and surely he did not need to push his tongue into my mouth. He did it so quickly that I had no time to move. The illustrator started other scenes.

The male model said, 'I have been a model for ten years now. I don't know why they always want young girls. Young girls have no experience and no expression. In Europe young girls of your age, under twenty, do not interest anyone. They are left in school or at home. They only become interesting after marriage.'

As he talked, I thought of Stephen. I thought of us at the beach, lying on the hot sand. I knew that Stephen loved me. I wanted him to take me. I wanted now to be made a woman quickly. I did not like being a virgin, always defending myself. I felt that everyone knew I was a virgin and was all the more keen to conquer me.

That evening Stephen and I were going out together. Somehow or other I must tell him. I must tell him that I was in danger of being raped, that he'd better do it first. No, he would then be so anxious. How could I tell him?

I had news for him. I was the star model now. I had more work than anyone else in the club, there were more demands for me because I was a foreigner and had an unusual face. I often had to pose in the evenings. I told Stephen all this. He was proud of me.

'You like your posing?' he said.

'I love it. I love to be with painters, to see them work – good or bad, I like the atmosphere of it, the stories I hear. It is varied, never the same. It is really adventure.'

'Do they . . . do they make love to you?' Stephen asked.

'Not if you don't want them to.'

'But do they try . . . ?'

I saw that he was anxious. We were walking to my house from the railway station, through the dark fields. I turned to him and offered my mouth. He kissed me. I said, 'Stephen, take me, take me, take me.'

He was completely dumbfounded. I was throwing myself into the refuge of his big arms, I wanted to be taken and have it all over with, I wanted to be made woman. But he was absolutely still, frightened. He said, 'I want to marry you, but I can't do it just now.'

'I don't care about the marriage.'

But now I became conscious of his surprise, and it quieted me. I was immensely disappointed by his conventional attitude. The moment passed. He thought it was merely an attack of blind passion, that I had lost my head. He was even proud to have protected me against my own impulses. I went home to bed and sobbed.

One illustrator asked me if I would pose on Sunday, that he was in a great rush to finish a poster. I consented. When I arrived he was already at work. It was morning and the building seemed deserted. His studio was on the thirteenth floor. He had half of the poster done. I got undressed quickly and put on the evening dress he had given me to wear. He did not seem to pay any attention to me. We worked in peace for a long while. I grew tired. He noticed it and gave me a rest. I walked about the studio looking at the other pictures. They were mostly portraits of actresses. I asked him who they were. He answered me with details about their sexual tastes:

'Oh, this one, this one demands romanticism. It's the only way you can get near her. She makes it difficult. She is European and she likes an intricate courtship. Halfway through I gave it up. It was too strenuous. She was very beautiful though, and there is something wonderful about getting a woman like that in bed. She had beautiful eyes, an entranced air, like some Hindu mystic. It makes you wonder how they will behave in bed.

'I have known other sexual angels. It is wonderful to

see the change in them. These clear eyes that you can see through, these bodies that take such beautiful harmonious poses, these delicate hands . . . how they change when desire takes hold of them. The sexual angels! They are wonderful because it is such a surprise, such a change. You, for instance, with your appearance of never having been touched, I can see you biting and scratching . . . I am sure your very voice changes – I have seen such changes. There are women's voices that sound like poetic, unearthly echoes. Then they change. The eyes change. I believe that all these legends about people changing into animals at night – like the stories of the werewolf, for instance – were invented by men who saw women transform at night from idealized, worshipful creatures into animals and thought that they were possessed. But I know it is something much simpler than that. You are a virgin, aren't you?'

'No, I am married,' I said.

'Married or not, you are a virgin. I can tell. I am never deceived. If you are married, your husband has not made you a woman yet. Don't you regret that? Don't you feel you are wasting time, that real living begins with sensation, with being a woman . . . ?'

This corresponded so exactly to what I had been feeling, to my desire to enter experience, that I was silent. I hated to admit this to a stranger.

I was conscious of being alone with the illustrator in an empty studio building. I was sad that Stephen had not understood my desire to become a woman. I was not frightened but fatalistic, desiring only to find someone I might fall in love with.

'I know what you are thinking,' he said, 'but for me it would not have any meaning unless the woman wanted me. I never could make love to a woman if she did not want me. When I first saw you, I felt how wonderful it would be to initiate you. There is something about you that makes me feel you will have many love affairs. I would like to be the first one. But not unless you wanted it.'

I smiled. 'That is exactly what I was thinking. It can only be if I want it, and I do not want it.'

'You must not give that first surrender so much importance. I think that was created by the people who wanted to preserve their daughters for marriage, the idea that the first man who takes a woman will have complete power over her. I think that is a superstition. It was created to help preserve women from promiscuity. It is actually untrue. If a man can make himself be loved, if he can rouse a woman, then she will be attracted to him. But the mere act of breaking through her virginity is not enough to accomplish this. Any man can do this and leave the woman unaroused. Did you know that many Spaniards take their wives this way and give them many children without completely initiating them sexually just to be sure of their faithfulness? The Spaniard believes in keeping pleasure for his mistress. In fact, if he sees a woman enjoy sensuality, he immediately suspects her of being faithless, even of being a whore.'

The illustrator's words haunted me for days. Then I was faced with a new problem. Summer had come and the painters were leaving for the country, for the beach, for far-off places in all directions. I did not have the money to follow them, and I was not sure how much work I would get. One morning I posed for an illustrator named Ronald. Afterwards he set the phonograph going and asked me to dance. While we were dancing he said, 'Why don't you come to the country for a while? It will do you good, you will get plenty of work, and I will pay for your trip. There are very few good models there. I am sure you will be kept busy.'

So I went. I took a little room in a farmhouse. Then I went to see Ronald, who lived down the road in a shed, into which he had built a huge window. The first thing he did was to blow his cigarette smoke into my mouth. I coughed.

'Oh,' he said, 'you don't know how to inhale.'

'I'm not at all interested,' I said, getting up. 'What kind of pose do you want?'

'Oh,' he said laughing, 'We don't work so hard here. You will have to learn to enjoy yourself a little. Now, take the smoke from my mouth and inhale it . . .'

'I don't like to inhale.'

He laughed again. He tried to kiss me. I moved away.

'Oh, oh,' he said, 'you are not going to be a very pleasant companion for me. I paid for your trip, you know, and I'm lonely down here. I expected you to be very pleasant company. Where is your suitcase?'

'I took a room down the road.'

'But you were invited to stay with me,' he said.

'I understood you wanted me to pose for you.'

'For the moment it is not a model I need.'

I started to leave. He said, 'You know, there is an understanding here about models who do not know how to enjoy themselves. If you take this attitude nobody will give you any work.'

I did not believe him. The next morning I began to knock on the doors of all the artists I could find. But Ronald had already paid them a visit. So I was received without cordiality, like a person who has played a trick on another. I did not have the money to return home, nor the money to pay for my room. I knew nobody. The country was beautiful, mountainous, but I could not enjoy it.

The next day I took a long walk and came upon a log cabin by the side of a river. I saw a man painting there, out of doors. I spoke to him. I told him my story. He did not know Ronald, but he was angry. He said he would try to help me. I told him all I wanted was to earn enough to return to New York.

So I began to pose for him. His name was Reynolds. He was a man of thirty or so, with black hair, very soft black eyes and a brilliant smile – a recluse. He never went to the village, except for food, nor frequented the restaurants or bars. He had a lax walk, easy gestures. He had been on the sea, always on tramp steamers, working as a sailor so that he could see foreign countries. He was always restless.

He painted from memory what he had seen in his travels. Now he sat at the foot of a tree and never looked around him but painted a wild piece of South American jungle.

Once when he and his friends were in the jungle,

Reynolds told me, they had smelled such a strong animal odor they thought they would suddenly see a panther, but out of the bushes had sprung with incredible velocity a woman, a naked savage woman, who looked at them with the frightened eyes of an animal, then ran off, leaving this strong animal scent behind her, threw herself into the river and swam away before they could catch their breath.

A friend of Reynolds had captured a woman like this. When he had washed off the red paint with which she was covered, she was very beautiful. She was gentle when well treated, succumbed to gifts of beads and ornaments.

Her strong smell repelled Reynolds until his friend had offered to let him have a night with her. He had found her black hair as hard and bristly as a beard. The animal smell made him feel he was lying with a panther. And she was so much stronger than he that after a while, he was acting almost like a woman, and she was the one who was molding him to suit her fancies. She was indefatigable and slow to arouse. She could bear caresses that exhausted him, and he fell asleep in her arms.

Then he found her climbing over him and pouring a little liquid over his penis, something that at first made him smart and then aroused him furiously. He was frightened. His penis seemed to have filled with fire, or with red peppers. He rubbed himself against her flesh, more to ease the burning than out of desire.

He was angry. She was smiling and laughing softly. He began taking her with a rage, driven by a fear that what she had done to him would arouse him for the last time, that it was some sort of enchantment to get the maximum of desire from him, until he died.

She lay back laughing, her white teeth showing, the animal odor of her now affecting him erotically like the smell of musk. She moved with such vigor that he felt she would tear his penis away from him. But now he wanted to subjugate her. He caressed her at the same time.

She was surprised by this. No one seemed to have done this to her before. When he was tired of taking her, after two orgasms, he continued to rub her clitoris, and she enjoyed this, begging for more, opening her legs wide. Then suddenly she turned over, crouched on the bed and swung her ass upward at an incredible angle. She expected him to take her again, but he continued to caress her. After this it was always his hand that she sought. She rubbed against it like a huge cat. During the day, if she met him she would rub her sex against his hand, surreptitiously.

Reynolds said that that night had made white women seem weak to him. He was laughing as he told the story.

His painting had reminded him of the savage woman hiding in the bushes, waiting like a tigress to leap and run away from the men who carried guns. He had painted her in, with her heavy, pointed breasts, her fine, long legs, her slender waist.

I did not know how I could pose for him. But he was thinking of another picture. He said, 'It will be easy. I want you to fall asleep. But you will be wrapped in white sheets. I saw something in Morocco once that I always wanted to paint. A woman had fallen asleep among her silk spools, holding the silk weaving frame with her hennaed feet. You have beautiful eyes, but they'll have to be closed.'

He went into the cabin and brought out sheets which he draped around me like a robe. He propped me against a wooden box, arranged my body and hands as he wanted them and began to sketch immediately. It was a very hot day. The sheets made me warm, and the pose was so lazy that I actually fell asleep, I don't know for how long. I felt languid and unreal. And then I felt a soft hand between my legs, very soft, caressing me so lightly I had to awaken to make sure I had been touched. Reynolds was bending over me, but with such an expression of delighted gentleness that I did not move. His eyes were tender, his mouth half open.

'Only a caress,' he said, 'just a caress.'

I did not move. I had never felt anything like this hand softly, softly caressing the skin between my legs without touching my sex. He only touched the tips of my pubic hair. Then his hand slipped down to the little valley around the sex. I was growing lax and soft. He leaned over and put his mouth on mine, lightly touching my lips, until my own mouth responded, and only then did he touch the tip of my tongue with his. His hand was moving, exploring, but so softly, it was tantalizing. I was wet, and I knew if he moved just a little more he would feel this. The languor spread all through my body. Each time his tongue touched mine I felt as if there were another little tongue inside of me, flicking out, wanting to be touched too. His hand moved only around my sex, and then around my ass, and it was as if he magnetized the blood to follow the movements of his hands. His finger touched the clitoris so gently, then slipped between the lips of the vulva. He felt the wetness. He touched this with delight, kissing me, lying over me now, and I did not move. The warmth, the smells of plants around me, his mouth over mine affected me like a drug.

'Only a caress,' he repeated gently, his finger moving around my clitoris until the little mound swelled and hardened. Then I felt as if a seed were bursting in me, a joy that made me palpitate under his fingers. I kissed him with gratitude. He was smiling. He said, 'Do you want to caress me?'

I nodded yes, but I did not know what he wanted of me. He unbuttoned his pants and I saw his penis. I took it in my hands. He said, 'Press harder.' He saw then that I did not know how. He took my hand in his and guided me. The little white foam fell all over my hand. He covered himself. He kissed me with the same grateful kiss I had given him after my pleasure.

He said, 'Did you know that a Hindu makes love to his wife ten days before he takes her? For ten days they merely caress and kiss.'

The thought of Ronald's behavior angered him all over again – the way he had wronged me in everybody's eyes. I said, 'Don't get angry. I am happy he did it, because it made me walk away from the village and come here.'

'I loved you as soon as I heard you speak with that

accent you have. I felt as if I were traveling again. Your face is so different, your walk, your ways. You remind me of the girl I intended to paint in Fez. I saw her only once, asleep like this. I always dreamed of awakening her as I awakened you.'

'And I always dreamed of being awakened with a caress like this,' I said.

'If you had been awake I might not have dared.'

'You, the adventurer, who lived with a savage woman?'

'I did not really live with the savage woman. That happened to a friend of mine. He was always talking about it, so I always tell it as if it had happened to me. I'm really timid with women. I can knock men down and fight and get drunk, but women intimidate me, even whores. They laugh at me. But this happened exactly as I had always planned it would happen.'

'But the tenth day I will be in New York,' I said laughing.

'The tenth day I will drive you back, if you have to go back. But meanwhile you are my prisoner.'

For ten days we worked out in the open, lying in the sun. The sun would warm my body, as Reynolds waited for me to close my eyes. Sometimes I pretended I wanted him to do more to me. I thought that if I closed my eyes he would take me. I liked the way he would walk up to me, like a hunter, making no sound and lying at my side. Sometimes he lifted my dress first and looked at me for a long time. Then he would touch me lightly, as if he did not want to awaken me, until the moisture came. His fingers would quicken. We kept our mouths together, our tongues caressing. I learned to take his penis in my mouth. This excited him terribly. He would lose all his gentleness, push his penis into my mouth, and I was afraid of choking. Once I bit him, hurt him, but he did not mind. I swallowed the white foam. When he kissed me, our faces were covered with it. The marvelous smell of sex impregnated my fingers. I did not want to wash my hands.

I felt that we shared a magnetic current, but at the same time nothing else bound us together. Reynolds had promised to drive me back to New York. He could not stay in the country much longer. I had to find work.

During the drive back Reynolds stopped the car and we lay on a blanket in the woods, resting. We caressed. He said, 'Are you happy?'

'Yes.'

'Can you continue to be happy, this way? As we are?'

'Why, Reynolds, what is it?'

'Listen, I love you. You know that, but I can't take you. I did that to a girl once, and she got pregnant and had an abortion. She bled to death. Since then I haven't been able to take a woman. I'm afraid. If that should happen to you, I would kill myself.'

I had never thought of things like this. I was silent. We kissed for a long time. For the first time he kissed me between the legs instead of caressing me, kissed me until I felt the orgasm. We were happy. He said, 'This little wound women have . . . it frightens me.'

In New York it was hot and all the artists were still

away. I found myself without work. I took up modeling in dress shops. I could easily get work, but when they asked me to go out in the evenings with the buyers I would refuse and lose the job. Finally I was taken into a big place near Thirty-fourth Street where they employed six models. This place was frightening and gray. There were long rows of clothes and a few benches for us to sit on. We waited in our slips, to be ready for quick changes. When our numbers were called, we helped one another dress.

The three men who sold the dress designs often tried to fondle us, squeeze us. We took turns staying during the lunch hour. My greatest fear was that I would be left alone with the man who was most persistent.

Once when Stephen telephoned to ask if he could see me that evening, the man came up behind me and put his hand into my slip to feel my breasts. Not knowing what else to do, I kicked him while I held the phone and tried to go on talking to Stephen. He was not discouraged. Next, he tried to feel my ass. I kicked again.

Stephen was saying, 'What is it, what are you saying?'

I ended the conversation and turned on the man. He was gone.

The buyers admired our physical qualities as much as the dresses. The head salesman was very proud of me and would often say, with his hand on my hair, 'She's an artist's model.'

This made me long to return to posing. I did not

want Reynolds or Stephen to find me here in an ugly office building, wearing dresses for ugly salesmen and buyers.

Finally I was called to model at the studio of a South American painter. He had the face of a woman, pale with big black eyes, long black hair, and his gestures were languid and effete. His studio was beautiful – luxuriant rugs, large paintings of nude women, silk hangings; and there was incense burning. He said he had a very intricate pose to do. He was painting a big horse running away with a naked woman. He asked if I had ever ridden on horseback. I said that I had, when I was younger.

'That is marvelous,' he said, 'exactly what I want. Now, I have made a contraption here which gives me the effect I need.'

It was a dummy of a horse without a head, just the body and legs, with a saddle.

He said, 'Take your clothes off first, then I will show you. I have difficulty with this part of the pose. The woman is throwing her body back because the horse is running wild, like this.' He sat on the dummy horse to show me.

By now I no longer felt timid about posing nude. I took my clothes off and sat on the horse, throwing my body backwards, my arms flying, my legs clasping the horse's flanks so as not to fall. The painter approved. He moved away and looked at me. 'It's a hard pose and I do not expect you to keep it long. Just let me know when you get tired.'

He studied me from every side. Then came up close to me and said, 'When I made the drawing, this part of the body showed clearly, here, between the legs.' He touched me lightly as if it were merely part of his work. I curved in my belly a little to throw the hips forward and then he said, 'Now it is fine. Hold it.'

He began to sketch. As I sat there I realized that there was one uncommon detail about the saddle. Most saddles, of course, are shaped to follow the contour of the ass and then rise at the pommel, where they are apt to rub against a woman's sex. I had often experienced both the advantages and the disadvantages of being supported there. Once my garter came loose from the stocking and began to dance around inside my riding trousers. My companions were galloping and I did not want to fall behind, so I continued. The garter, leaping in all directions, finally fell between my sex and the saddle and hurt me. I held on, gritting my teeth. The pain was strangely mixed with a sensation I could not define. I was a girl then and did not know anything about sex. I thought that a woman's sex was inside of her, and I did not know about the clitoris.

When the ride was over, I was in pain. I mentioned what had happened to a girl I knew well, and we both went into the bathroom. She helped me out of my trousers, out of my little belt with the garters on it, and then said, 'Are you hurt? That's a very sensitive spot. Maybe you'll never have any pleasure there if you got hurt.'

I let her look at it. It was red and a little swollen, but not so very painful. What bothered me was her saying I might be deprived of a pleasure by this, a pleasure I did not know. She insisted on bathing it with a wet cotton, fondled me and finally kissed me, 'to make it well'.

I became acutely aware of this part of my body. Particularly when we rode a long while in the heat, I felt such a warmth and stirring between my legs that all I desired was to get off the horse and let my friend nurse me again. She was always asking me, 'Does it hurt?'

So once I answered, 'Just a little.' We dismounted and went into the bathroom, and she bathed the chaffed spot with cotton and cool water.

And again she fondled me, saying, 'But it does not look sore anymore. Maybe you will be able to enjoy yourself again.'

'I don't know,' I said. 'Do you think it has gone . . . dead . . . from the pain?'

My friend very tenderly leaned over and touched me. 'Does it hurt?'

I lay back and said, 'No, I do not feel anything.'

'Don't you feel this?' she asked with concern, pressing the lips between her fingers.

'No,' I said, watching her.

'Don't you feel this?' She passed her fingers now around the tip of the clitoris, making tiny circles.

'I don't feel anything.'

She became eager to see if I had lost my sensibility and increased her caresses, rubbing the clitoris with one hand while she vibrated the tip with the other. She stroked my pubic hair and tender skin around it.

Finally I felt her, wildly, and I began to move. She was panting over me, watching me and saying, 'Wonderful, wonderful, you can feel there . . .'

I was remembering this as I sat on the dummy horse and noticed that the pommel was quite accentuated. So the painter could see what he wanted to paint, I slid forward, and as I did so my sex rubbed against the leather prominence. The painter was observing me.

'Do you like my horse?' he said. 'Do you know that I can make it move?'

'Can you?'

He came near me and set the dummy in motion, and indeed it was perfectly constructed to move like a horse.

'I like it,' I said. 'It reminds me of the times I rode horseback when I was a girl.' I noticed that he stopped painting now to watch me. The motion of the horse pushed my sex against the saddle even harder and gave me great pleasure. I thought that he would notice it, and so I said, 'Stop it now.' But he smiled and did not stop it. 'Don't you like it?' he said.

I did like it. Each movement brought the leather against my clitoris, and I thought I could not hold back an orgasm if it went on. I begged him to stop. My face was flushed.

The painter was carefully watching me, watching every expression of a pleasure I could not control, and now it increased so that I abandoned myself to the motion of the horse, let myself rub against the leather, until I felt the orgasm and I came, riding this way in front of him.

Only then did I know that he expected it, that he had done all this to see me enjoy it. He knew when to stop the machinery. 'You can rest now,' he said.

Soon after, I went to pose for a woman illustrator, Lena, I had met at a party. She liked company. Actors and actresses came to see her, writers. She painted for magazine covers. The door was always open. People brought drinks. The talk was acid, cruel. It seemed to me that all her friends were caricaturists. Everyone's weaknesses were immediately exposed. Or they exposed their own. One beautiful young man, dressed with great elegance, made no secret of his profession. He sat around at the big hotels, waited for old women who were alone and took them out to dance. Very often they invited him back to their rooms.

Lena made a wry face, 'How can you do it?' she asked him, 'Such old women, how can you possibly get an erection? If I saw a woman like that lying on my bed, I would run away.'

The young man smiled. 'There are so many ways of doing it. One is to close my eyes and to imagine it is not an old woman but a woman I like, and then when my eyes are closed I begin to think how pleasant it will be to be able to pay my rent the next day or to buy a new suit or silk shirts. And as I do this, I keep stroking the woman's sex without looking, and, you know, if your eyes are closed, they feel about the same, more or less. Sometimes, though, when I have difficulty I take drugs. Of course, I know that at this rate my career will last about five years and that at the end of that time I will not be of any use even to a young woman. But by then I will be glad never to see a woman again.

'I certainly envy my Argentine friend, my roommate. He is a handsome, aristocratic man, absolutely effete. Women would love him. When I leave the apartment, do you know what he does? He gets up out of bed, pulls out a small electric iron and an ironing board, takes his pants and begins to press them. As he presses them he imagines how he will come out of the building so impeccably dressed, how he will walk down Fifth Avenue, how somewhere he will spy a beautiful woman, follow the scent of her perfume for many blocks, follow her into crowded elevators, almost touching her. The woman will be wearing a veil and a fur around her neck. Her dress will outline her figure.

'After following her thus through the shops, he will finally speak to her. She will see his handsome face smiling at her and the chivalrous way he has of carrying himself. They will go off together and sit having tea somewhere, then go to the hotel where she is staying. She will invite him to come up with her. They will get into the room and then pull down the shades and lie in the darkness making love.

'As he presses his pants carefully, meticulously, my friend imagines how he will make love to this woman – and it excites him. He knows how he will grip her. He likes to push his penis in from behind and raise the woman's legs, and then get her to turn just a little so that he can see it moving in and out. He likes the woman to squeeze the base of his penis at the same time; her fingers press harder than the mouth of her sex, and that excites him. She will also touch his balls as he moves, and he will touch her clitoris, because that gives her a double pleasure. He will make her gasp and shake from head to foot and beg for more.

'By the time he has envisioned all this standing there, half naked, pressing his pants, my friend has a hard on. It is all he wants. He puts away the pants, the iron and the ironing board, and he gets into bed again, lying back and smoking, thinking over this scene until each detail of it is perfect and a drop of semen appears at the head of his penis, which he strokes while he lies smoking and dreaming of pursuing other women.

'I envy him because he can get so much excitement from thinking all this. He questions me. He wants to know how my women are made, how they behave . . .'

Lena laughed. She said, 'It's hot. I will take my corset off.' And she went into the alcove. When she came back her body looked free and lax. She sat down, crossed her bare legs, her blouse half-open. One of her friends sat where he could see her.

Another one, a handsome man, stood near me as I was posing and whispered compliments. He said, 'I love you because you remind me of Europe — Paris especially. I don't know what there is about Paris, but there is sensuality in the air there. It is contagious. It is such a human city. I don't know whether it is because couples are always kissing in the streets, at tables in the cafés, in the movies, in the parks. They embrace each other so freely. They stop for long complete kisses in the middle of the sidewalk, at the subway entrances. Perhaps it is that, or the softness of the air. I don't know. In the dark, in each doorway at night there is a man and a woman almost melted into one another. The whores watch for you every moment . . . they touch you.

'One day I was standing on a platform bus, looking up idly at the houses. I saw a window open and a man and woman lying on a bed. The woman was sitting over the man.

'At five o'clock in the afternoon it becomes unbearable. There is love and desire in the air. Everybody is in the streets. The cafés are full. In the movies there are little boxes that are completely dark and curtained off so that you can make love on the floor while the movie is going on and not be seen. It is all so open, so easy. No police to interfere. A woman friend of mine who was followed and annoyed by a man complained to the policeman at the corner. He laughed and said, "You'll be sorrier the day no man wants to annoy you, won't you? After all, you should be thankful instead of getting angry." And he would not help her.'

Then my admirer said in a lower voice, 'Will you come and have dinner with me and go to the theatre?'

He became my first real lover. I forgot Reynolds and Stephen. They now seem like children to me.

Hilda and Rango

Hilda was a beautiful Parisian model who fell deeply in love with an American writer, whose work was so violent and sensual that it attracted women to him immediately. They would write him letters or try for an introduction through his friends. Those who succeeded in meeting him were always amazed by his gentleness, his softness.

Hilda had the same experience. Seeing that he remained impassive, she began to court him. It was only when she had made the first advances, caressed him, that he began making love to her as she had expected to be made love to. But each time, she would have to begin all over. First she had to tempt him in some way — fix a loosened garter, or talk about some experience in the past, or lie on his couch, throw back her head and thrust her breasts forward, stretching herself like an enormous cat. She would sit on his lap, offer her mouth, unbutton his pants, excite him.

They lived together for several years, deeply attached to each other. She became accustomed to his sexual rhythm. He lay back waiting and enjoying himself. She learned to be active, bold, but she suffered, because she was by nature extraordinarily feminine. Deep down she had the belief that woman could easily control her desire, but that man could not, that it was even harmful for him to try to. She felt that woman was meant to respond to man's desire. She had always dreamed of having a man who would force her will, rule her sexually, lead.

She gratified this man because she loved him. She learned to seek out his penis and touch it until he was aroused, to seek his mouth and stir his tongue, to press her body against his, to incite him. Sometimes they would be lying down and talking. She would place her hand over his penis and find it hard. Yet he made no move towards her. Slowly then, she became used to expressing her own desire, her own moods. She lost all her reserve, her timidity.

One night at a party in Montparnasse, she met a Mexican painter, a huge dark man with heavy charcoal eyes, eyebrows and hair. He was drunk. She was to discover that he was almost always drunk.

But the sight of her gave him a profound shock. He pulled himself up from his faltering, tottering posture and faced her as if he were a big lion facing a tamer. Something about her made him stand still and try to become sober again, to rise from the fog and fumes in which he lived continuously. Something about her face made him stand ashamed of his unkempt clothes, the paint under his nails, the uncombed black hair. She, on the other hand, was struck by this image of a demon, the demon she had imagined to exist behind the work of the American writer.

He was huge, restless, destructive, loved no one, was attached to nothing, a tramp and an adventurer. He would paint at the studios of friends, borrowing oils and canvas, then leave his work there and go off. Most of the time he lived with the gypsies on the outskirts of Paris. With them he shared their life in the gypsy carts, traveling all through France. He respected their laws, never made love to the gypsy women, played the guitar with them at night clubs when they needed money, ate their meals – very often made of stolen chicken.

When he met Hilda, he had his own gypsy cart just outside one of the gates of Paris, near the ancient barricades, which were now crumbling. The cart had belonged to a Portuguese who had covered its walls with painted leather. The bed was hung at the back of the cart, suspended like a ship's bunk. The windows were arched. The ceiling was so low it was difficult for one to stand up.

At the party that first evening, Rango did not invite Hilda to dance, although friends of his were providing the music for the night. The lights in the studio had been put out because enough light came from the street, and couples stood on the balcony with their arms around each other. The music was languid and dissolving.

Rango stood above Hilda and stared at her. Then he said, 'Do you want to walk?' Hilda said yes. Rango walked with his hands in his pockets, a cigarette dangling from the corner of his mouth. He was sober now, his head as clear as the night. He was walking towards the outskirts of the city. They came to the rag-pickers' shacks, little shacks built unevenly, crazily, with sloping roofs and no windows – enough air came through the cracked boards and badly built doors. The paths were made of earth.

A little farther on stood a row of gypsy carts. It was four in the morning, and people were asleep. Hilda did not talk. She walked in the shadow of Rango with a great feeling of being taken out of herself, of having no will and no knowledge of what was happening to her, merely a pervading sense of flow.

Rango's arms were bare. Hilda was aware of only one thing, that she wanted these bare arms to grip her. He bowed to enter his cart. He lit a candle. He was too tall for the low ceiling, but she was smaller and could stand straight.

The candles made huge shadows. His bed was open, merely a blanket thrown back. His clothes were strewn around. There were two guitars. He took one up and began to play, sitting among his clothes. Hilda had the feeling that she was dreaming, that she must keep her eyes on his bare arms, on his throat showing through the open shirt, so that he would feel what she felt, the same magnetism.

At the same moment that she felt she was falling into darkness, into his golden-brown flesh, he fell towards her, covered her with kisses, very hot, quick kisses, into which his breath passed. He kissed her behind her ears, on her eyelids, her throat, her shoulders. She was blinded, deafened, made senseless. Every kiss, like a gulp of wine, added to the warmth of her body. Every kiss increased the heat of his lips. But he made no gesture to raise her dress or to undress her.

They lay there for a long time. The candle was

finished. It sputtered and went out. In the darkness she felt his burning dryness, like desert sand, enveloping her.

Then in this darkness, the Hilda who had made this gesture so many times before was impelled to make it once more, out of her dream and drunkenness of kisses. Her hand fumbled for his belt with the cold silver buckle, felt below the belt at the buttons of his pants, felt his desire.

Suddenly he pushed her away, as if she had wounded him. He stood up, reeling a little, and lit another candle. She could not understand what had happened. She saw that he was angry. His eyes had grown fierce. His high cheeks, which seemed always to be smiling, no longer smiled. His mouth was compressed.

'What have I done?' she asked.

He looked like some wild, timid animal that one had done violence to. He looked humiliated, offended, proud, untouchable. She repeated, 'What have I done?' She knew that she had done something she ought not to have done. She wanted him to understand that she was innocent.

He smiled now, ironically, at her blindness. He said, 'You made the gesture of a whore.' A deep shame, a sense of great injury overwhelmed her. The woman in her that had suffered from being forced to act as she did with her other lover, the woman who had been made to betray her real nature so often that it had become a habit, this woman wept now, uncontrollably. The tears did not touch him. She got up, saying, 'Even if it is the last time I come here, there is something

I want you to know. A woman does not always do what she wants. I was taught by someone . . . someone I have lived with for a number of years and who forced me . . . forced me to act . . .'

Rango listened. She continued. 'I suffered at first, I changed my whole nature . . . I . . .' Then she stopped.

Rango sat down next to her. 'I understand.' He took up his guitar. He played for her. They drank. But he did not touch her. They walked slowly back to where she lived. She dropped exhausted on her bed and fell asleep weeping, not only for the loss of Rango but for the loss of that part of herself she had deformed, changed for love of a man.

The next day Rango was waiting for her at the door of her little hotel. He stood there reading and smoking. When she came out, he said simply, 'Come and have coffee with me.' They sat at the Martinique Café, a café frequented by mulattos, prize fighters, drug addicts. He had chosen a dark corner of the café, and now he bent over her and began to kiss her. He did not pause. He kept her mouth on his and did not move. She dissolved in this kiss.

They walked the streets like Parisian apaches, kissing continuously, making their way to his gypsy cart, half unconscious. Now in full daylight, the place was alive with gypsy women preparing to sell lace in the market. Their men slept. Others were preparing to travel south. Rango said he had always wanted to go with them. But he had a job playing guitar at a night club where they paid him well.

'And now,' he said, 'I have you.'

In the cart he offered her wine and they smoked. And he kissed her again. He raised himself to close the little curtain. And then he undressed her, slowly, taking off the stockings delicately, his big brown hands handling them as if they were gauze, invisible. He stopped to look at her garters. He kissed her feet. He smiled at her. His face was strangely pure, illumined with a youthful joy, and he undressed her as if she were his first woman. He was awkward with her skirt but finally unhooked it, with a curiosity about the way it fastened. More adeptly he raised her sweater above her head, and she was left with only her panties on. He fell on her, kissing her mouth over and over again. Then he took off his own clothes, and fell on her again. As they kissed, his hand gripped her panties and pulled them, and he whispered, 'You are so delicate, so small. I cannot believe that you have a sex.' He parted her legs only to kiss her. She felt his penis hard against her belly, but he took it and pushed it downwards.

Hilda was amazed to see him do this, push his penis down between his legs, cruelly, thrusting away his desire. It was as if he enjoyed denying himself, while at the same time arousing them both to a breaking point with kissing.

Hilda moaned with the pleasure and the pain of expectancy. He moved over her body, now kissing her mouth, now her sex, so that the shell-like flavor of the sex was brought to her mouth and they mingled together, in his mouth and breath.

But he continued to push away his penis, and when

they had worn themselves out with unfulfilled excitement he lay over her and fell asleep like a child, his fists closed, his head on her breasts. Now and then he caressed her, mumbling, 'It is not possible that you have a sex. You are too delicate and small . . . You are unreal . . .' He kept his hand between her legs. She rested against his body, which was twice the size of hers. She was vibrating so much that she could not sleep.

His body smelled like a precious-wood forest; his hair, like sandalwood, his skin, like cedar. It was as if he had always lived among trees and plants. Lying at his side, deprived of her fulfillment, Hilda felt that the female in her was being taught to submit to the male, to obey his wishes. She felt that he was still punishing her for the gesture she had made, for her impatience, for her first act of leadership. He would rouse and deprive her until he had broken this willfulness in her.

Had he understood that it was involuntary, not truly in her? Whether he had or not, he was blindly determined to break her. Over and over again they met, undressed, lay side by side, kissed and caressed themselves to a frenzy, and each time he pushed his penis downwards and hid it away.

Over and over again she lay passive, showing no desire, no impatience. She was in a state of excitement, which exacerbated all her sensibilities. It was as if she had taken new drugs that made the entire body more alive to caresses, to a touch, to the very air. She felt her dress on her skin like a hand. It seemed to her that everything was touching her like a hand, teasing her breasts, her thighs continuously. She had discovered a new realm, a realm of suspense and watchfulness, of erotic wakefulness such as she had never known.

One day when she was walking with him, she lost the heel of one shoe. He had to carry her. That night he took her, in the candlelight. He was like a demon crouching over her, his hair wild, his charcoal-black eyes burning into hers, his strong penis pounding into her, into the woman whose submission he first demanded, submission to his desire, his hour.

Two Sisters

There were two young sisters. One was stocky, dark-haired, vivid. The other was graceful, delicate. Dorothy had strength. Edna had a beautiful voice that haunted people, and she wanted to be an actress. They came from a well-to-do family who lived in Maryland. In the cellar of their house their father made a ceremony of burning D. H. Lawrence's books, which betrays how far behind this family was in the development of the sensual life. In spite of this, their father, with his eyes wet and brilliant, liked to take the girls on his knees, slip his hand under their little dresses and caress them.

They had two brothers, Jake and David. Before the boys could get an erection they played at making love with their sisters. David and Dorothy were always paired off together, as were Edna and Jake. The delicate David liked his husky sister, and the rather virile Jake liked the plantlike fragility of Edna. The brothers laid their soft young penises between their sisters' legs, but that was all. This was done in great secrecy, lying on the rug of the dining room and accompanied by a feeling that they were committing the greatest of sexual crimes.

Then suddenly these games stopped. The boys had discovered the world of sex through another boy. The sisters became self-conscious and were growing up.

Puritanism was asserting itself in the family. Their father thundered and fought each intrusion from the outside world. He growled at the young men who came to call. He growled at dances, at parties of all kinds. With the fanaticism of an inquisitor, he burned the books he found his children reading. He gave up caressing his daughters. He did not know that they had made slits in their panties so when they dated they could be kissed between the legs, and they sat in cars with boys, sucking their penises, that the seat of the family car was stained with sperm. Even so, he fought off the young men who called too often. He did everything to prevent his daughters from marrying.

Dorothy was studying sculpture. Edna still wanted to go on the stage. But then she fell in love with a man older than herself, the first man she had really known. The others were boys to her; they aroused a sort of maternal craving in her, a desire to protect. But Harry was forty, and he worked for a company that took rich people on cruises. As social captain of the cruise, it was his job to see that the guests were entertained, that they met one another, that their comforts were complete – and their intrigues, too. He helped the husbands to escape the vigilance of the wives, and the wives to escape their husbands. His stories of trips with these pampered rich stirred Edna.

They got married. They took a trip around the world together. What Edna discovered in their travels was that the social captain supplied a great deal of the sexual intrigue in person.

Edna returned from the trip estranged from her

husband. Sexually he had not awakened her. She did not know why. Sometimes she thought it was because of her discovery of his having belonged to so many women. From the first night, it seemed that his possession was not of her, but of a woman like a hundred others. He had shown no emotion. When he undressed her he had said, 'Oh, you have such thick hips. You seemed so slender, I never imagined you could have such thick hips.'

She felt humiliated, she felt that she was not desirable. This paralyzed her own confidence, her own outflow of love and desire for him. Partly in a mood of revenge, she began to look at him just as coldly as he had looked at her, and what she saw was a man of forty whose hair was growing thin, who was soon going to be very fat and looked ready to retire into a familiar and stolid life. He was no longer the man who had seen all the world.

Then came Robert, thirty years old, dark-haired, with burning brown eyes like some animal that looked at once hungry and tender. He was fascinated by Edna's voice, enchanted by the softness of it. He was completely spellbound by her.

He had just won a scholarship with an acting company. He and Edna shared a love of the stage. He renewed her faith in herself, in her attractiveness. He was not even quite aware that it was love. He treated her somewhat like an older sister, until one day backstage, when everyone had gone home and Edna had been rehearsing him, listening to him, giving her impressions, they acted out a kiss that did not stop. He took her, on the sofa of the stage setting, awkwardly, hurriedly, but with such an intensity that she felt him as she had never felt her husband. His words of praise, worship, cries of wonder, incited her, and she bloomed in his hands. They fell on the floor. The dust got into their throats, but they were still kissing, caressing, and Robert had a second erection.

Edna and Robert were together all the time. Her alibi for Harry was that she was studying acting. It was a period of drunkenness, of blindness, of living only with the hands and mouth and body. Edna let Harry go off alone on his cruise. She was free now for six months. She and Robert lived together in New York, secretly. He had such magnetism in his hands that his touch, even his hand on her arm, sent warmth through her. She lived open and sensitized to his presence. And his feeling about her voice was the same. He would telephone her at all hours to hear it. It was like a song luring him out of himself and out of his life. All other women were canceled by her voice.

He entered her love with a sense of absolute possession, security. To hide and sleep in her, take her, enjoy her, they were all the same. There were no tensions, no moments of ambivalence, hatred. The lovemaking never became wild and cruel, an animal bout in which one strives to rape the other, force one's way into the other and hurt with violence and desire. No, this was a melting together, a vanishing into a soft, dark womb of warmth.

Harry returned. And at the same time Dorothy came back from the West, where she had been working, sculpturing. She was herself now like a piece of highly polished wood, her features firm and chiseled, her voice earthy, her legs sturdy, her very nature hard and strong, like the work she did.

She saw what had happened to Edna but did not know about her estrangement from Harry. She thought Robert had caused it, and hated him. She assumed he was a lover of the moment, just separating Harry and Edna for his own pleasure. She did not believe it was love. She fought Robert. She was cutting, biting. She herself was like an impregnable virgin, though not puritanical or squeamish. She was open like a man, used lusty words, told bawdy stories, laughed about sex. But still she was impregnable to all.

She felt Robert's antagonism exultantly. She loved the fire and angry demons in him, biting, snarling at her. What she hated above all was that most men in her presence wilted, grew small and feeble. Only the timid ones approached her, as if to seek her strength. She wanted to shatter them, seeing the way they crawled towards her treelike body. The idea of letting them push their penis between her legs was like allowing some insect to crawl over her. Whereas she gloried in the struggle to push Robert out of Edna's life, to humiliate him, demolish him. The three of them would sit together, Edna hiding her feelings about Harry, Robert not offering to take her away, not thinking, living only in the romantic present – dreamer. Dorothy accused him of this. Edna defended him; all the time she sat there thinking of the fiery way Robert took her the first time, the narrow little couch on which they lay, the dusty rug on which they rolled; thinking of his hands, the way they penetrated her.

Edna said to her sister, 'You cannot understand. You have never been in love like this.'

Then Dorothy was silenced.

The two sisters slept in adjoining rooms. There was a big bathroom between the rooms. Harry had gone again for six months. Edna let Robert come to her room at night.

One morning looking out of the window, Dorothy saw Edna leave the house. She did not know that Robert was still in her room asleep. She went into the bathroom to take a bath. Edna had left her door open, and Dorothy, thinking herself alone, did not trouble to close it. On this door there was a mirror. Dorothy came into the bathroom and dropped her kimono. She pinned her hair up, she made up her face. Her body was magnificent. Every movement she made before the mirror brought out the provocative full, taut curve of her breasts and buttocks. Her hair was full of lights; she brushed it. Her breasts danced as she moved. She stood on her toes to make up her eyelashes.

And Robert, on awakening, found himself looking at this spectacle from the bed, everything mirrored before him. Suddenly his whole body flushed with warmth. He threw off the covers. Dorothy was still visible in the mirror. She was leaning over to pick up her hairbrush. Robert could not bear any more. He went to the bathroom and stood there. Dorothy made no outcry. He was naked, his penis thrust out towards her, his brown eyes burning her.

As he made a step towards her, Dorothy was taken with a strange trembling. She felt herself craving to move towards him. They fell upon each other. He half dragged, half carried her to the bed. It was like the continuation of their struggle, for she fought him, but her every movement only made him increase the pressure of his knees, of his hands, of his mouth. Robert was wild with a desire to hurt, to bend her to his will, her resistance warming his muscles, his anger. As he took her, breaking through the virginity, he bit into her, adding pain. She was oblivious to it because of the effect of his body on hers. Wherever he touched her, she burned; after the initial pain it seemed as if her womb was inflamed too. When it was over, she craved him again. It was she who took his penis between her hands and pushed it in again, and stronger than the pain was the ecstasy of his moving inside of her.

Robert had discovered a stronger sensation, a stronger flavor – the smell of Dorothy's hair, of her body, the strength of her as she enclosed him. In one hour she had obliterated his feelings for Edna.

Afterwards, Dorothy was like one possessed as she remembered Robert lying over her body, moving up so that he could rub his penis between her breasts, moving towards her mouth, and she felt the dizziness one experiences before an abyss, a sense of falling, of annihilation.

She did not know how to face Edna. She was torn with jealousy. She was afraid Robert would try to keep them both. But with Edna he only felt like becoming a child, lying at her side, putting his head on her breast and confessing everything to her, out of a need for a mother, not thinking at all of the hurt it would cause her. But he realized he could not stay. He invented a trip. He begged Dorothy to go with him. Dorothy said she would leave later. He went to London.

Edna followed him there. Dorothy went to Paris. She was now trying to escape Robert because of her love for Edna. She began having an affair with a young American, Donald, because he resembled Robert.

Robert wrote her that he could not make love to Edna any more, that he had to pretend all the time. He had found out she was born the same day as his mother, and she was becoming more and more identified with his mother, which paralyzed him. He wouldn't tell her the truth.

Soon after, he went to Paris to meet Dorothy. She continued to see Donald, too. Then she and Robert went on a trip. That week together, they thought they were going to go crazy. Robert's caresses put Dorothy in such a state that she begged, 'Take me!' He would pretend to refuse, just to see her rolling in exquisite torture, on the verge of an orgasm and needing him only to touch her with the tip of his penis. Then she learned to tease him, too, to leave him when he was about to come. She would pretend to fall asleep. And he would lie there, tortured by the desire to be touched again, afraid to awaken her. He would edge close to her, place his penis against her ass, trying to move against it, to come just by touching her, but he couldn't and then she would awaken and begin touching him and sucking him again. They did it so often that it became a torture. Her face was swollen from the kissing, and she had marks of his teeth on her body, and yet they could not touch each other in the street, even while out walking, without jumping again with desire.

They decided to get married. Robert wrote to Edna.

On the day of the wedding, Edna came to Paris. Why? It was as if she wanted to see everything with her own eyes, to suffer the very last drop of bitterness. In a few days she had become an old woman. A month before she was glowing, enchanting, her voice like a song, like an aureola around her, her walk light, her smile inundating one. And now she wore a mask. Over this mask she had spread powder. There was no glow of life under it. Her hair was lifeless. The glaze in her eyes was like that of a dying person.

Dorothy was faint when she saw her. She cried out to her. Edna did not answer. She merely stared.

The wedding was ghostly. Donald burst in in the middle of it and behaved like a madman, threatening Dorothy for deceiving him, threatening to commit suicide. When it was over, Dorothy fainted. Edna stood there carrying flowers, a figure of death.

Robert and Dorothy left on a trip. They wanted to revisit the places they had traveled through a few weeks before, recapture the same pleasure. But when Robert tried to take Dorothy he found that she could not respond. Her body had undergone a change. The life had ebbed from it. He thought, It is the strain, the strain of having seen Edna, of the wedding, the scene made by Donald. So he was tender. He waited. Dorothy wept during the night. The next night it was the same. And the next. Robert tried caressing her, but her body did not vibrate under his fingers. Even her mouth did not answer his mouth. It was as though she had died. After a while she concealed it from him. She pretended to feel enjoyment. But when Robert was not looking at her, she looked exactly like Edna on the day of the wedding.

She kept her secret. Robert was deceived, until one day when they took a room in a rather cheap hotel, because the best ones were filled. The walls were thin, the doors did not close well. They got into bed. As soon as they put out the light they heard the springs of the bed in the next room squeaking rhythmically, two heavy bodies pounding into each other. Then the woman began to moan. Dorothy sat up in bed and sobbed for all that was lost.

Obscurely she felt what had happened to be a punishment. She knew it was related to her taking Robert from Edna. She thought she could recapture at least the physical response with other men, and perhaps free herself and return to Robert. When they went back to New York she sought adventures. In her head she was always hearing the moans and cries of the couple in the hotel room. She would not rest until she had felt this again. Edna could not cheat her of this, could not kill the life in her. It was too great a punishment for something that was not altogether her fault.

She tried to meet Donald again. But Donald had changed. He had hardened, crystallized. Once an emotional, impulsive young man, he had become completely objective, mature, searching for his pleasure.

'Of course,' he said to Dorothy, 'you know who is responsible for this. I would not have minded at all if you had discovered you didn't love me, left me, gone to Robert. I knew you were attracted to him, I didn't know how deeply. But I couldn't forgive you keeping us both at the same time, in Paris. I must have taken you often a few minutes after he had. You asked for violence. I didn't know you were asking me to surpass Robert, to try to efface him from your body. I thought you were merely in a frenzy of desire. So I responded. You know how I made love to you, I cracked your bones, I bent you, I twisted you. Once I made you bleed. Then from me you would take a taxi and go to him. And you told me that after lovemaking you didn't wash because you liked the smell that went through your clothes, you liked the smells that followed you for a day after. I nearly went crazy when I discovered all this, I wanted to kill you.'

'I have been sufficiently punished,' said Dorothy violently.

Donald looked at her. 'What do you mean?'

'Ever since I married Robert I have been frigid.'

Donald's eyebrows lifted. Then his face set in an ironical expression. 'And why do you tell me this? Do you expect me to make you bleed again? So that you can go back to your Robert all wet between the legs, and enjoy him at last? God knows I still love you. But my life is changed. I do not go in for love any more.'

'How do you live?'

'I have my little pleasures. I invite certain choice

friends; I offer them drinks; they sit in my room – where you are sitting. Then I go into the kitchen to mix more drinks, and give them a little time alone. They already know my taste, my little predilections.

'When I come back . . . well, she may be sitting in your armchair with her skirt lifted, and he kneeling before her looking at her or kissing her, or he may be sitting in the chair and she . . .

'What I like is the surprise, and seeing them. They do not notice me. In a way, that is how it would have been with you and Robert if I could have witnessed your little scenes. Possibly a remembrance of some kind. Now if you like, you can wait a few minutes. There is a friend coming. He is exceptionally attractive.'

Dorothy wanted to leave. Then she observed something that made her stop. The door of Donald's bathroom was open. It was covered with a mirror. She turned to Donald and said: 'Listen, I'll stay, but can I express a whim, too? One that will not in the least alter the satisfaction of yours.'

'What is it?'

'Instead of going into the kitchen when you leave us, will you go into the bathroom for a while, and look at the mirror?'

Donald consented. His friend, John, arrived. He was a magnificent man physically, but in his face there was a strange quality of decadence, a laxity about the eyes and mouth, something on the verge of perverseness, which fascinated Dorothy. It was as if none of the ordinary pleasures of love could satisfy him. In his face there was a peculiar insatiability, curiosity – he had something of the animal. His lips bared his teeth. He seemed startled at the sight of Dorothy.

'I like women of fine breed,' he said immediately and looked gratefully at Donald for the gift, the surprise of her presence.

Dorothy was all in fur from head to toe – hat, muff, gloves, even fur on her shoes. Her perfume had already filled the room.

John stood above her, smiling. His gestures were growing more festive. Suddenly he bent forward like some stage director and said: 'I have something to ask you. You are so beautiful. I hate the clothes which conceal a woman. Yet I hate to take them off. Will you do something for me, something exceptionally wonderful? Please take your clothes off in the other room and come back in here in only your furs. Will you? I'll tell you why I ask you this. Only thoroughbred women look beautiful in furs, and you are a thoroughbred.'

Dorothy went into the bathroom, slipped out of her clothes and returned in her furs, keeping on only her stockings and little fur trimmed shoes.

John's eyes glittered with pleasure. He could only sit and look at her. His excitement was so strong and contagious that Dorothy began to feel her breasts growing sensitive at the tips. She had a feeling that she wanted to expose them, that she wanted to open the fur and watch John's pleasure. Usually the warmth and the stirring of the nipples occurred together with the warmth and stirring of the sex mouth. Today she could feel only her breasts, the compulsion to expose them, to raise them with her hands, to offer them. John leaned over and put his mouth to them.

Donald had left. He waited in the bathroom and looked into the mirror of the door. He saw Dorothy standing by John, her breasts in her hands. The fur had opened to reveal her whole body, glowing, luminous, rich in the fur, like some jeweled animal. Donald was stirred. John did not touch the body, he sucked at the breasts, sometimes stopping to feel the fur with his mouth, as if he were kissing a beautiful animal. The odor of her sex — pungent shell and sea odors, as if woman came out of the sea as Venus did — mixed with the odor of the fur, and John's suckling grew more violent. Seeing Dorothy in the mirror, seeing the hair of her sex like the hair of the fur, Donald felt that if John touched her between the legs he would strike him. He came out of the bathroom, his penis exposed and erect, and walked towards Dorothy. This was so much like the first scene of her passion for Robert that she moaned with joy, tore herself from John and turned fully upon Donald, saying: 'Take me, take me!'

Closing her eyes, she imagined Robert crouching over her, tigerlike, tearing open the fur, and caressing her with many hands and mouths and tongues, touching every part of her, parting her legs, kissing her, biting her, licking her. She incited the two men to a frenzy. Nothing was heard but the breathing, the little suckling sounds, the sound of the penis swimming in her moisture.

Leaving them both drowsy, she dressed and went so quickly that they were barely aware of it. Donald cursed: 'She couldn't wait. She couldn't wait, she had to go back to him just as before. All wet and juicy from other men's lovemaking.'

It was true that Dorothy did not wash. When Robert arrived home a few moments after, she was filled with rich odors, open, vibrating still. Her eyes, her gestures, her languid pose on the couch invited him. Robert knew her moods. He was quick to respond to them. He was so happy that she was as she had been long ago. She would be moist between the legs now, responsive. He plunged into her.

Robert was never quite certain of when she was coming. The penis is rarely aware of this spasm in a woman, this little palpitation. The penis can feel only its own ejaculation. This time Robert wanted to feel the spasm in Dorothy, the wild little clutching. He withheld his orgasm. She was convulsed. The moment seemed to have come. He forgot his watching in his own wave of pleasure. And Dorothy carried off her deception, unable to reach the orgasm that she had had only an hour before while closing her eyes and pretending it was Robert who was taking her.

Linda

Linda stood in front of her mirror examining herself critically in full daylight. Now past thirty, she was becoming concerned with her age, although nothing about her betrayed any lessening of her beauty. She was slender, youthful in appearance. She could well deceive everyone but herself. In her own eyes her flesh was losing some of its firmness, some of that marble smoothness that she had admired so often in her own mirror.

She was no less loved. If anything she was more loved than ever, because now she attracted all the young men who sense that it is from such a woman that they will really learn the secrets of lovemaking, and who feel no attraction to the young girls of their age who are backward, innocent, inexperienced, and still possessed by their families.

Linda's husband, a handsome man of forty, had loved her with the fervor of a lover for many years. He closed his eyes to her young admirers. He believed that she did not take them seriously, that her interest was due to her childlessness and the need to pour her protective feelings over people who were beginning to live. He himself was reputed to be a seducer of women of all classes and character.

She remembered that on her wedding night André

had been an adoring lover, worshiping each part of her body separately, as if she were a work of art, touching her and marveling, commenting on her ears, her feet, her neck, her hair, her nose, her cheeks, and her thighs, as he fondled them. His words and voice, his touch, opened her flesh like a flower to the heat and light.

He trained her to be a sexually perfect instrument, to vibrate to every form of caress. One time he taught her to put the rest of her body to sleep, as it were, and to concentrate all her erotic feelings in her mouth. Then she was like a woman half-drugged, lying there, her body quiet and languid, and her mouth, her lips, became another sex organ.

André had a particular passion for her mouth. In the street he looked at women's mouths. To him the mouth was indicative of the sex. A tightness of a lip, thinness, augured nothing rich or voluptuous. A full mouth promised an open, generous sex. A moist mouth tantalized him. A mouth that opened out, a mouth that was parted as if ready for a kiss, he would follow doggedly in the street until he could possess the woman and prove again his conviction of the revelatory powers of the mouth.

Linda's mouth had seduced him from the first. It had a perverse, half-dolorous expression. There was something about the way she moved it, a passionate unfolding of the lips, promising a person who would lash around the beloved like a storm. When he first saw Linda, he was taken into her through this mouth, as if he were already making love to her. And so it was on their wedding night. He was obsessed with her mouth. It was on her mouth that he threw himself, kissing it until it burned, until the tongue was worn out, until the lips were swollen; and then, when he had fully aroused her mouth, it was thus that he took her, crouching over her, his strong lips pressed against her breasts.

He never treated her as a wife. He wooed her over and over again, with presents, flowers, new pleasures. He took her to dinner at the *cabinets particuliers* of Paris, to the big restaurants, where all the waiters thought she was his mistress.

He chose the most exciting food and wine for her. He made her drunk with his caressing words. He made love to her mouth. He made her say that she wanted him. Then he would ask: 'And how do you want me? What part of you wants me tonight?'

Sometimes she answered, 'My mouth wants you, I want to feel you in my mouth, way down in my mouth.' Other times she answered, 'I am moist between the legs.'

This is how they talked across restaurant tables, in the small private dining rooms created especially for lovers. How discreet the waiters, knowing when not to return. Music would come from an invisible source. There would be a divan. When the meal was served, and André had pressed Linda's knees between his and stolen kisses, he would take her on the divan, with her clothes on, like lovers who do not have time to undress.

He would escort her to the opera and to the theaters famed for their dark boxes, and make love to her while they watched a spectacle. He would make love to her in taxis, in a barge anchored in front of Notre Dame that rented cabins to lovers. Everywhere but at home, on the marital bed. He would drive her to little far-off villages and stay at romantic inns with her. He would take a room for them in the luxurious houses of prostitution he had known. Then he would treat her like a prostitute. He would make her submit to his whims, ask to be whipped, ask her to crawl on her hands and knees and not to kiss him but to pass her tongue all over him like an animal.

These practices had aroused her sensuality to such a degree that she was frightened. She was afraid of the day when André would cease to be sufficient for her. Her sensuality was, she knew, vigorous; his was the last burst of a man who had spent himself on a life of excess and now gave her the flower of it.

A day came when André had to leave her for ten days for a trip. Linda was restless and feverish. A friend telephoned her, André's friend, the painter of the day in Paris, the favorite of all women. He said to her, 'Are you bored with yourself, Linda? Would you care to join us in a very special kind of party? Do you have a mask?'

Linda knew exactly what he meant. She and André had often laughed at Jacques's parties in the Bois. It was his favorite form of amusement: on a summer night, to gather society people wearing masks, drive to the Bois with bottles of champagne, find a clearing in the wooded section and disport themselves.

She was tempted. She had never participated in one. That, André had not wanted to do. He said playfully that the question of the masks might confuse him and that he did not want to make love to the wrong woman.

Linda accepted the invitation. She put on one of her new evening dresses, a heavy satin dress which outlined her body like a wet glove. She wore no underwear, no jewelry that could identify her. She changed her hair style, from a page-boy frame around her face to a pompadour style, which revealed the shape of her face and neck. Then she tied the black mask on her face, pinning the elastic to her hair for greater security.

At the last minute she decided to change the color of her hair and had it washed and tinted blue-black instead of pale blond. Then she put it up again and found herself so altered that it startled her.

About eighty people had been asked to meet at the big studio of the fashionable painter. It was dimly lit so as to preserve the guests' identities better. When they were all there, they were whisked to the waiting automobiles. The chauffeurs knew where to go. In the deepest part of the woods there was a beautiful clearing covered with moss. There they sat, having sent the chauffeurs away, and began to drink champagne. Many of the caresses had already begun in the crowded automobiles. The masks gave people a liberty that turned the most refined ones into hungry animals. Hands ran under the sumptuous evening dress to touch what they wanted to touch, knees intertwined, breaths came quicker.

Linda was pursued by two men. The first of them did all he could to arouse her by kissing her mouth and breasts, while the other, with more success, caressed her legs under her long dress, until she revealed by a shudder that she was aroused. Then he wanted to carry her off into the darkness.

The first man protested but was too drunk to compete. She was carried away from the group to where the trees made dark shadows and lowered onto the moss. From nearby there were cries of resistance, there were grunts, there was a woman shrieking, 'Do it, do it, I can't wait any more, do it, do it to me!'

The orgy was in full bloom. Women caressed one another. Two men would set about teasing a woman into a frenzy and then stop merely to enjoy the sight of her, with her dress half-undone, a shoulder strap fallen, a breast uncovered, while she tried to satisfy herself by pressing obscenely against the men, rubbing against them, begging, lifting her dress.

Linda was astonished by the bestiality of her aggressor. She, who had known only the voluptuous caresses of her husband, found herself now in the grip of something infinitely more powerful, a desire so violent it seemed devouring.

His hands gripped her like claws, he lifted her sex to meet his penis as if he did not care if he broke her bones in doing so. He used *coups de bélier*, truly like a horn entering her, a goring that did not hurt but which made her want to retaliate with the same fury. After he had satisfied himself once with a wildness and violence that stunned her, he whispered, 'Now I want you to satisfy yourself, fully, do you hear me? As you never did before.' He held his erect penis like a primitive wooden symbol, held it out for her to use as she wished.

He incited her to unleash her most violent appetite on him. She was hardly aware of biting into his flesh. He panted in her ears, 'Go on, go on, I know you women, you never really let yourself take a man as you want to.'

From some depths of her body that she had never known, there came a savage fever that would not spend itself, that could not have enough of his mouth, his tongue, his penis inside of her, a fever that was not content with an orgasm. She felt his teeth buried in her shoulder, as her teeth bit into his neck, and then she fell backward and lost consciousness.

When she awakened, she was lying on an iron bed in a shabby room. A man was asleep beside her. She was naked, and he too, but half-covered by the sheet. She recognized the body which had crushed her the night before in the Bois. It was the body of an athlete, big, brown, muscular. The head was handsome, strong, with wild hair. As she looked at him admiringly, he opened his eyes and smiled.

'I could not let you go back with the others, I might never have seen you again,' he said.

'How did you get me here?'

'I stole you.'

'Where are we?'

'In a very poor hotel, where I live.'

'Then you're not . . .'

'I'm not a friend of the others, if that is what you mean. I am simply a workman. One night, bicycling back from my work, I saw one of your *partouzes*. I got undressed and joined it. The women seemed to enjoy me. I was not discovered. When I had made love to them, I stole away. Last night I was passing by again and I heard the voices. I found you being kissed by that man, and I carried you off. Now I have brought you here. It may make trouble for you, but I could not give you up. You're a real woman, the others are feeble compared to you. You've got fire.'

'I have to leave,' said Linda.

'But I want your promise that you will come back.'

He sat up and looked at her. His physical beauty gave him a grandeur, and she vibrated at his nearness. He began to kiss her and she felt languid again. She put her hand on his hard penis. The joys of the night before were still running through her body. She let him take her again almost as if to make sure that she had not dreamed. No, this man who could make his penis burn through her whole body and kiss her as if it were to be the last kiss, this man was real.

And so Linda returned to him. It was the place where she felt most alive. But after a year she lost him. He fell in love with another woman and married her. Linda had become so accustomed to him that now everyone else seemed too delicate, too refined, too pale, feeble. Among the men she knew, there was none with that savage strength and fervor of her lost lover. She searched for him again and again, in small bars, in the lost places of Paris. She met prizefighters, circus stars, athletes. With each she tried to find the same embraces. But they failed to arouse her.

When Linda lost the workman because he wanted to have a woman of his own, a woman to come home to, a woman who would take care of him, she confided in her hairdresser. The Parisian hairdresser plays a vital role in the life of a French woman. He not only dresses her hair, about which she is particularly fastidious, but he is an arbiter of fashion. He is her best critic and confessor in matters of love. The two hours that it takes to get one's hair washed, curled and dried is ample time for confidences. The seclusion of the little cabinet protects secrets.

When Linda had first arrived in Paris from the little town in the South of France where she was born and she and her husband had met, she was only twenty years old. She was badly dressed, shy, innocent. She had luxuriant hair which she did not know how to arrange. She used no make-up. Walking down the Rue Saint-Honoré admiring the shop windows, she became fully aware of her deficiences. She became aware of what the famous Parisian chic meant, that fastidiousness of detail which made of any woman a work of art. Its purpose was to heighten her physical attributes. It was created largely by the skill of the dressmakers. What no other country was ever able to imitate was the erotic quality of French clothes, the art of letting the body express all its charms through clothes.

In France they know the erotic value of heavy black satin, giving the shimmering quality of a wet naked body. They know how to delineate the contours of the breast, how to make the folds of the dress follow the movements of the body. They know the mystery of veils, of lace over the skin, of provocative underwear, of a dress daringly slit.

The contour of a shoe, the sleekness of a glove, these give the Parisian woman a trimness, an audacity, that far surpasses the seductiveness of other women. Centuries of coquetry have produced a kind of perfection that is apparent not only in the rich women but in the little shop girls. And the hairdresser is the priest of this cult for perfection. He tutors the women who come from the provinces. He refines vulgar women; he brightens pale women; he gives them all new personalities.

Linda was fortunate enough to fall into the hands of Michel, whose salon was near the Champs Elysées. Michel was a man of forty, slender, elegant and rather feminine. He spoke suavely, had beautiful salon manners, kissed her hand like an aristocrat, kept his little mustache pointed and glazed. His talk was bright and alive. He was a philosopher and a creator of women. When Linda came in, he cocked his head like a painter who is about to begin a work of art.

After a few months Linda emerged a polished product. Michel became, besides, her confessor and director. He had not always been a hairdresser of well-to-do women. He did not mind telling that he had begun in a very poor quarter where his father was a hairdresser. There the women's hair was spoiled by hunger, by cheap soaps, carelessness, rough handling.

'Dry as a wig,' he said. 'Too much cheap perfume. There was one young girl – I have never forgotten her. She worked for a dressmaker. She had a passion for perfume but could not afford any. I used to keep the last of the toilet water bottles for her. Whenever I gave a woman a perfume rinse, I saw to it that a little was left in the bottle. And when Gisele came I liked to pour it down between her breasts. She was so delighted that she did not notice how I enjoyed it. I would take the collar of her dress between my thumb and forefinger, pull it out a little, and drop the perfume down, stealing a glance at her young breasts. She had a voluptuous way of moving afterward, of closing her eyes and taking in the smell and reveling in it. She would cry out sometimes, "Oh, Michel, you've wet me too much this time." And she would rub her dress against her breasts to dry herself.

'Then once I could not resist her any more. I dropped the perfume down her neck, and when she threw her head back and closed her eyes, my hand slipped right to her breasts. Well, Gisele never came back.

'But that was only the beginning of my career as a perfumer of women. I began to take the task seriously. I kept perfume in an atomizer and enjoyed spraying it on the breasts of my clients. They never refused that. Then I learned to give them a little brushing after they were ready. That's a very enjoyable task, dusting the coat of a well-formed woman.

'And some women's hair puts me in a state which I cannot describe to you. It might offend you. But there are women whose hair smells so intimate, like musk, that it makes a man – well, I cannot always keep myself under control. You know how helpless women are when they are lying back to have their hair washed, or when they are under the dryer, or having a permanent.'

Michel would look a client over and say, 'You could

easily get fifteen thousand francs a month,' which meant an apartment on the Champs Elysées, a car, fine clothes, and a friend who would be generous. Or she might become a woman of the first category, the mistress of a senator or of the writer or actor of the day.

When he helped a woman reach the position due her, he maintained her secret. He never talked about anybody's life except in disguised terms. He knew a woman married for ten years to the president of a big American corporation. She still had her prostitute's card and was well known to the police and to the hospitals where the prostitutes went for weekly examinations. Even today, she could not become altogether accustomed to her new position and at times forgot that she had the money in her pocket to tip the men who waited on her during her Clipper trip across the ocean. Instead of a tip she handed out a little card with her address.

It was Michel who counseled Linda never to be jealous, that she must remember there were more women in the world than men, especially in France, and that a woman must be generous with her husband – think how many women would be left without a knowledge of love. He said this seriously. He thought of jealousy as a sort of miserliness. The only truly generous women were the prostitutes, actresses, who did not withhold their bodies. To his mind, the meanest type of woman was the American gold digger who knew how to extract money from men without giving herself, which Michel thought a sign of bad character.

He thought that every woman should at one time or

another be a whore. He thought that all women, deep down, wished to be a whore once in their lives and that it was good for them. It was the best way to retain a sense of being a female.

When Linda lost her workman, therefore, it was natural for her to consult Michel. He advised her to take up prostitution. That way, he said, she would have the satisfaction of proving to herself that she was desirable entirely apart from the question of love, and she might find a man who would treat her with the necessary violence. In her own world she was too worshiped, adored, spoiled, to know her true value as a female, to be treated with the brutality that she liked.

Linda realized that this would be the best way to discover whether she was aging, losing her potency and charms. So she took the address Michel gave her, got into a taxi and was taken to a place on the Avenue du Bois, a private house with a grandiose appearance of seclusion and aristocracy. There she was received without questions.

'*De bonne famille?*' That was all they wanted to ascertain. This was a house which specialized in women *de bonne famille.* Immediately the caretaker would telephone a client: 'We have a newcomer, a woman of most exquisite refinement.'

Linda was shown into a spacious boudoir with ivory furniture, brocade draperies. She had taken off her hat and veil and was standing before the large gold-framed mirror arranging her hair, when the door opened.

The man who came in was almost grotesque in appearance. He was short and stout, with a head too big for his body, features like an overgrown child's, too soft and hazy and tender for his age and bulk. He walked very swiftly toward her and kissed her hand ceremoniously. He said, 'My dear, how wonderful it is that you were able to escape from your home and husband.'

Linda was about to protest when she became aware of the man's desire to pretend. Immediately she fell into the role but trembled within herself at the thought of yielding to this man. Already her eyes were turning towards the door, and she wondered if she could make her escape. He caught her glance and said very quickly, 'You need not be afraid. What I ask of you is nothing to be frightened about. I am grateful to you for risking your reputation to meet me here, for leaving your husband for me. I ask very little, this presence of yours here makes me very happy. I have never seen a woman more beautiful than you are, and more aristocratic. I love your perfume, and your dress, your taste in jewelry. Do let me see your feet. What beautiful shoes. How elegant they are, and what a delicate ankle you have. Ah, it is not very often that so beautiful a woman comes to see me. I have not been lucky with women.'

Now it seemed to her that he looked more and more like a child, everything about him, the awkwardness of his gestures, the softness of his hands. When he lit a cigarette and smoked, she felt that this must be his first cigarette, because of the awkward way he handled it and the curiosity with which he watched the smoke.

'I cannot stay very long,' she said, impelled by the need to escape. This was not at all what she had expected.

'I will not keep you very long. Will you let me see your handkerchief?'

She offered him a delicate, perfumed handkerchief. He smelled it with an air of extreme pleasure.

Then he said, 'I have no intention of taking you as you expect me to. I am not interested in possessing you as other men do. All I ask of you is that you pass this handkerchief between your legs and then give it to me, that is all.'

She realized that this would be so much easier than what she had feared. She did it willingly. He watched her as she leaned over, raised her skirt, unfastened the lace pants and passed the handkerchief slowly between her legs. He leaned over then and put his hand over the handkerchief merely to increase the pressure and so that she would pass it again.

He was trembling from head to foot. His eyes were dilated. Linda realized that he was in a state of great excitement. When he took the handkerchief away he looked at it as if it were a woman, a precious jewel.

He was too absorbed to talk. He walked over to the bed, laid the handkerchief on the bedspread and then threw himself on it, unbuttoning his trousers as he fell. He pushed and rubbed. After a moment he sat up on the bed, wrapped his penis with the handkerchief and then continued jerking, finally reaching an orgasm which made him cry out with joy. He had completely forgotten Linda. He was in a state of ecstasy. The handkerchief was wet from his ejaculation. He lay back panting.

Linda left him. As she walked through the hallways

of the house she met the woman who had received her. The woman was amazed that she should want to leave so soon. 'I gave you one of our most refined clients,' she said, 'a harmless creature.'

It was after this episode that Linda sat in the Bois one day watching the parade of spring costumes on a Sunday morning. She was drinking in the colors and elegance and perfumes when she became conscious of a particular perfume near her. She turned her head. To her right sat a handsome man of about forty, elegantly dressed, with his glossy black hair carefully combed back. Was it from his hair that this perfume came? It reminded Linda of her voyage to Fez, of the great beauty of the Arab men there. It had a potent effect on her. She looked at the man. He turned and smiled at her, a brilliant white smile of big strong teeth with two smaller milk teeth, slightly crooked, which gave him a roguish air.

Linda said, 'You use a perfume which I smelled in Fez.'

'That's right,' said the man, 'I was in Fez. I bought this at the market there. I have a passion for perfumes. But since I found this one I have never used any other.'

'It smells like some precious wood,' said Linda. 'Men should smell like precious wood. I have always dreamed of finally reaching a country in South America where there are whole forests of precious woods which exude marvelous odors. Once I was in love with patchouli, a very ancient perfume. People no longer use it. It came from India. The Indian shawls of our grandmothers were always saturated with patchouli. I like to walk along the docks, too, and smell spices in the ware-houses. Do you do that?'

'I do. I follow women sometimes, just because of their perfume, their smell.'

'I wanted to stay in Fez and marry an Arab.'

'Why didn't you?'

'Because I fell in love with an Arab once. I visited him several times. He was the handsomest man I had ever seen. He had a dark skin and enormous jet eyes, an expression of such emotion and fervor that it swept me off my feet. He had a thundering voice and the softest manner. Whenever he talked to anyone, he would stand, even in the street, holding their two hands, tenderly, as if he wanted to touch all human beings with the same great softness and tenderness. I was completely seduced, but . . .'

'What happened?'

'One day, when it was extremely hot, we sat drinking mint tea in his garden and he took off his turban. His head was completely shaved. It is the tradition of the Arabs. It seems that all their heads are completely shaved. That somehow cured me of my infatuation.'

The stranger laughed.

With perfect synchronization, they got up and started to walk together. Linda was as much affected by the perfume, which came from the man's hair, as she would have been by a glass of wine. Her legs felt unsteady, her head foggy. Her breasts swelled and fell with the deep breaths she took. The stranger watched the heaving of her breasts as if he were watching the sea unfolding at his feet.

At the edge of the Bois he stopped. 'I live right up there,' he said, pointing with his cane to an apartment with many balconies. 'Would you care to come in and have an apéritif with me on my terrace?'

Linda accepted. It seemed to her that, were she deprived of the perfume which enchanted her, she would suffocate.

They sat on his terrace, quietly drinking. Linda leaned back languidly. The stranger continued to watch her breasts. Then he closed his eyes. Neither of them made a movement. Both had fallen into a dream.

He was the first to move. As he kissed her Linda was carried back to Fez, to the garden of the tall Arab. She remembered her sensations of that day, the desire to be enfolded in the white cape of the Arab, the desire for his potent voice and his burning eyes. The smile of the stranger was brilliant, like the smile of the Arab. The stranger *was* the Arab, the Arab with thick black hair, perfumed like the city of Fez. Two men were making love to her. She kept her eyes closed. The Arab was undressing her. The Arab was touching her with fiery hands. Waves of perfume dilated her body, opened it, prepared her to yield. Her nerves were set for a climax, tense, responsive.

She half opened her eyes and saw the dazzling teeth about to bite into her flesh. And then his sex touched her and entered her. It was like something electrically charged, each thrust sending currents throughout her body.

He parted her legs as if he wanted to break them apart. His hair fell on her face. Smelling it, she felt the orgasm coming and called out to him to increase his thrusts so that they could come together. At the moment of the orgasm he cried out in a tiger's roar, a tremendous sound of joy, ecstasy and furious enjoyment such as she had never heard. It was as she had imagined the Arab would cry, like some jungle animal, satisfied with his prey, who roars with pleasure. She opened her eyes. Her face was covered with his black hair. She took it into her mouth.

Their bodies were completely tangled. Her panties had been so hurriedly pulled down that they had fallen the length of her legs and lay around her ankles, and he had somehow inserted his foot into one half of the panties. They looked at their legs bound together by this bit of black chiffon, and they laughed.

She returned many times to this apartment. Her desire would begin long before each meeting, as she dressed for him. At all hours of the day his perfume would issue from some mysterious source and haunt her. Sometimes as she was about to cross a street, she would remember his scent so vividly that the turmoil between her legs would make her stand there, helpless, dilated. Something of it clung to her body and disturbed her at night when she was sleeping alone. She had never been so easily aroused. She had always needed time and caresses, but for the Arab, as she called him to herself, it seemed as if she were always erotically prepared, so much so that she was aroused long before he touched her, and what she feared was that she would come at the very first touch of his finger on her sex.

That happened once. She arrived at his apartment moist and trembling. The lips of her sex were as stiff as if they had been caressed, her nipples hard, her whole body quivering, and as he kissed her he felt her turmoil and slipped his hand directly to her sex. The sensation was so acute that she came.

And then one day, about two months after their liaison, she went to him and when he took her in his arms she felt no desire. He did not seem to be the same man. As he stood in front of her she coldly observed his elegance and his ordinariness. He looked like any elegant Frenchman one could see walking down the Champs Elysées, or at opening nights, or at the races.

But what had changed him in her eyes? Why did she not feel this great intoxication she felt ordinarily in his presence? There was something so usual now about him. So like any other man. So unlike the Arab. His smile seemed less brilliant, his voice less colorful. Suddenly she fell into his arms and tried to smell his hair. She cried out, 'Your perfume, you have no perfume on!'

'It's finished,' said the Arab Frenchman. 'And I cannot get any like it. But why should that upset you so?'

Linda tried to recapture the mood he threw her into. She felt her body cold. She pretended. She closed her eyes and she began to imagine. She was in Fez again, sitting in a garden. The Arab was sitting at her side, on a low, soft couch. He had thrown her back on the couch and kissed her while the little water fountain sang in her ears, and the familiar perfume burned in an incense holder at her side. But, no. The fantasy was broken. There was no incense. The place smelled like a French apartment. The man at her side was a stranger. He was deprived of his magic that made her desire him. She never went to see him again.

Although Linda had not relished the adventure of the handkerchief, after a few months of not moving from her own sphere she became restless again.

She was haunted by memories, by stories she heard, by the feeling that everywhere around her men and women were enjoying sensual pleasure. She feared that now that she had ceased to enjoy her husband, her body was dying.

She remembered being sexually awakened by an accident at a very early age. Her mother had bought her panties that were too small for her and very tight between the legs. They had irritated her skin, and at night while falling asleep she had scratched herself. As she fell asleep, the scratching became softer and then she became aware that it was a pleasurable sensation. She continued to caress her skin and found that as her fingers came nearer the little place in the center, the pleasure increased. Under her fingers she felt a part which seemed to harden at her touch, and there found an even greater sensibility.

A few days later she was sent to confession. The priest sat at his chair and she was made to kneel at his feet. He was a Dominican and wore a long cord with a tassel which fell at his right side. As Linda leaned against his knees, she felt this tassel against her. The priest had a big warm voice which enveloped her, and he leaned down to talk to her. When she had finished with the ordinary sins – anger, lies and so on – she paused. Observing her hesitation, he began to whisper in a much lower tone, 'Do you ever have impure dreams?'

'What dreams, Father?' she asked.

The hard tassel that she felt just at the sensitive place between her legs affected her like her fingers' caresses of the nights before. She tried to move closer to it. She wanted to hear the voice of the priest, warm and suggestive, asking about the impure dreams. He said, 'Do you ever have dreams of being kissed, or of kissing someone?'

'No, Father.'

Now she felt that the tassel was infinitely more affecting than her fingers because, in some mysterious way or other, it was part of the priest's warm voice and his words, like 'kisses'. She pressed against him harder and looked at him.

He felt that she had something to confess, and asked, 'Do you ever caress yourself?'

'Caress myself how?'

The priest was about to dismiss the question, thinking his intuition had been an error, but the expression of her face confirmed his doubts.

'Do you ever touch yourself with your hands?'

It was at this moment that Linda wanted so much to be able to make one movement of friction and once again reach that extreme, overwhelming pleasure she had discovered a few nights ago. But she was afraid the priest would become aware and repulse her and she would lose the sensation completely. She was determined to hold his attention, and began, 'Father, it is true, I have something very terrible to confess. I scratched myself one night and then I caressed myself, and –'

'My child, my child,' said the priest, 'you must stop this immediately. It is impure. It will ruin your life.'

'Why is it impure?' asked Linda, pressing against the tassel. Her excitement was rising. The priest leaned over so close that his lips almost touched her forehead. She was dizzy. He said, 'Those are the caresses that only your husband can give you. If you do it and abuse them, you will grow weak, and no one will love you. How often have you done it?'

'For three nights, Father. I have had dreams too.'

'What sort of dreams?'

'I have had dreams of someone touching me there.'

Every word she said increased her excitement, and with a pretense of guilt and shame she threw herself against the priest's knees and bowed her head as if she would cry, but it was because the touch of the tassel had brought on the orgasm and she was shaking. The priest, thinking it was guilt and shame, took her in his arms, raised her from her kneeling position and comforted her.

The Ring

In Peru it is the custom among the Indians to exchange rings for a betrothal, rings that have been in their possession for a long time. These rings are sometimes in the shape of a chain.

A very handsome Indian fell in love with a Peruvian woman of Spanish descent, but there was violent opposition on the part of her family. The Indians were purported to be lazy and degenerate, and to produce weak and unstable children, particularly when married to Spanish blood.

In spite of the opposition, the young people carried out their engagement ceremony among their friends. The girl's father came in during the festivities and threatened that, if he ever met the Indian wearing the chain ring the girl had already given him, he would tear it from his finger in the bloodiest manner, and if necessary cut his finger off. The festivities were spoiled by this incident. Everybody went home, and the young people separated with promises to meet secretly.

They met one evening after many difficulties, and kissed fervently for a long while. The woman was exalted by his kisses. She was ready to give herself, feeling that this might be their last moment together, for her father's anger was growing every day. But the Indian was determined to marry her, determined not to possess her in secrecy. Then she noticed that he did not have the ring on his finger. Her eyes questioned him. He said in her ear, 'I am wearing it, but not where it can be seen. I am wearing it where no one can see it, but where it will prevent me from taking you or any other woman until we are married.'

'I don't understand,' said the woman. 'Where is the ring?'

Then he took her hand, led it to a certain place between the legs. The woman's fingers felt his penis first of all, and then he guided her fingers and she felt the ring there at the base of it. At the touch of her hand, however, the penis hardened and he cried out, because the ring pressed into it and gave him excruciating pain.

The woman almost fainted with horror. It was as if he wanted to kill and mutilate the desire in himself. And at the same time the thought of this penis bound and encircled by her ring roused her sexually, so that her body became warm and sensitive to all kinds of erotic fantasies. She continued to kiss him, and he begged her not to, because it brought him greater and greater pain.

A few days later the Indian was again in agony, but he could not get the ring off. The doctor had to be called, and the ring filed away.

The woman came to him and offered to run away with him. He accepted. They got on horses and traveled for a whole night together to a nearby town. There he concealed her in a room and went out to get work on an hacienda. She did not leave the room until her father tired of searching for her. The night watchman of the town was the only one aware of her presence. The watchman was a young man and had helped to conceal her. From her window she could see him walking back and forth carrying the keys of the houses, and calling, 'The night is clear and all is well in the town.'

When someone came home late he would clap his hands together and call for the watchman. The watchman would open the door. While the Indian was away at work the watchman and the woman chatted together innocently.

He told her about a crime that had recently taken place in the village. The Indians who left the mountain and their work on the haciendas and went down to the jungle became wild and beast-like. Their faces changed from lean, noble contours to bestial grossness.

Such a transformation had just taken place in an Indian who had once been the handsomest man of the village, gracious, silent, with a strange humor and a reserved sensuality. He had gone down to the jungle and made money hunting. Now he had returned. He was homesick. He came back poor and wandered about homeless. No one recognized or remembered him.

Then he had caught a little girl on the road and ripped her sexual parts with a long knife used for skinning animals. He had not violated her, but had taken the knife and inserted it into her sex, and bela-bored her with it. The whole village was in a turmoil. They could not decide how to punish him. A very old Indian practice was to be revived for his sake. His wounds would be parted and wax, mixed with a biting acid the Indians knew of, inserted into them so that the pain would be doubled. Then he was to be flogged to death.

As the watchman told this story to the woman, her lover returned from his work. He saw her leaning out of the window and looking at the watchman. He rushed up to her room and appeared before her with his black hair wild around his face, his eyes full of lightning bolts of anger and jealousy. He began to curse her and torture her with questions and doubts.

Ever since the accident with the ring his penis had remained sensitive. The lovemaking was accompanied with pain, and so he could not indulge in it as often as he wanted. His penis would swell and hurt him for days. He was always afraid he was not satisfying his mistress and that she might love another. When he saw the tall watchman talking to her, he was sure they were carrying on an affair behind his back. He wanted to hurt her, he wanted her to suffer bodily in some way, as he had suffered for her. He forced her to go downstairs with him to the cellar where the wines were kept in vats under beamed ceilings.

He tied a rope to one of the beams. The woman thought he was going to beat her. She could not understand why he was preparing a pulley. Then he tied her hands and began pulling on the rope so that her body was raised in the air and the whole weight of it hung on her wrists, and the pain was great.

She wept and swore that she had been faithful, but he was insane. When she fainted as he pulled the rope again, he came to his senses. He took her down and began embracing her and caressing her. She opened her eyes and smiled at him.

He was overcome with desire for her and he threw himself on her. He thought that she would resist him, that after the pain she had endured she would be angry. But she made no resistance. She continued to smile at him. And when he touched her sex he found that she was wet. He took her with fury, and she responded with the same exaltation. It was the best night they ever had together, lying there on the cold cellar floor in the darkness.